Dujardin-Beaumetz, E. P. Hurd

The modern treatment of diseases of the liver

Dujardin-Beaumetz, E. P. Hurd

The modern treatment of diseases of the liver

ISBN/EAN: 9783742828620

Manufactured in Europe, USA, Canada, Australia, Japa

Cover: Foto ©Andreas Hilbeck / pixelio.de

Manufactured and distributed by brebook publishing software
(www.brebook.com)

Dujardin-Beaumetz, E. P. Hurd

The modern treatment of diseases of the liver

THE MODERN TREATMENT

OF

DISEASES OF THE LIVER.

—BY—

PROF. DUJARDIN-BEAUMETZ,

*Member of the Academy of Medicine and of the Council of Hygiene
and Salubrity of the Seine; Editor of the Bulletin Général
de Therapeutique, Paris, France.*

TRANSLATED FROM THE FIFTH FRENCH EDITION BY

E. P. HURD, M. D.,

Newburyport, Mass.

1888.
GEORGE S. DAVIS,
DETROIT, MICH.

AUTHOR'S PREFACE.

Dr. Hurd, who in making known my works in the United States, has displayed a zeal and activity which I cannot too much praise, in this volume presents to the medical profession of the American Republic that part of the second volume of my Lecons de Clinique Thérapeutique which pertains to the treatment of diseases of the liver.

The hepatic diseases constitute an important chapter of internal pathology, and one which I have here endeavored succinctly to treat, epitomizing to my best ability the existing knowledge respecting this subject. I am aware that I have not given to this chapter all the extension and development which it deserves, and this is my reason: Utility being my main object, I have taken up only those diseases of the hepatic gland which we observe in our country, leaving one side all that important group of liver diseases which are so prevalent in tropical countries, and which the reader will find described at great length in leading text-books devoted to this subject.

I may venture to hope that physicians in the United States will accord to this volume the same welcome and the same indulgence which have been extended to my previous publications.

In concluding, I have to thank Mr. George S. Davis for the pains which he has taken in the typographical execution of these little volumes (for with the present I include the two volumes of last year's series on Diseases of the Heart), and I have especially to acknowledge my obligations to my friend and correspondent, Dr. Hurd, for the fidelity with which he has reproduced my lectures, preserving their original form, and making no more changes than the English idiom demands.

DUJARDIN-BEAUMETZ.

AUGUST 1, 1883.

TRANSLATOR'S PREFACE.

The works of Dr. Dujardin-Beaumetz, which have now appeared in English are the following, given in the order of their publication :

1. CLINICAL THERAPEUTICS (1885) (from the press of G. S. Davis, Detroit). An octavo of about 500 pages, comprehending the treatment of Nervous Diseases, General Diseases and Fevers. This is Vol. III of the Leçons de Clinique Thérapeutique.

2. ON BACTERIA (1885). This treatise, of about 100 pages, was published as an appendix to "Diseases of the Lungs of a Specific Character," by Germain Sée, and issued by Wm. Wood & Co., as the November number of the Library Series for 1885.

3. DISEASES OF THE STOMACH AND INTESTINES. This work, which is the second part of Vol. I, of the the Leçons de Clinique Thérapeutique, is an octavo of about 400 pages, and constitutes the May number of Wood's Library Series for 1886.

4. NEW MEDICATIONS. This is a volume of 320 pages, and is a part of Davis' Leisure Library Series for 1886.

5. ALIMENTARY HYGIENE. A treatise on the Dietetic Treatment of Disease. The various chapters of this work may be found in files of the Boston Medical and Surgical Journal, Medical News and Therapeutic Gazette (the latter principally) for the years 1886–1887.

6. THE MODERN TREATMENT OF DISEASES OF THE HEART.

7. THE MODERN TREATMENT OF DISEASES OF THE AORTA. These two volumes comprise the remainder of Vol. I of the Leçons de Clinique Thérapeutique, and constitute Nos. 2 and 4 of the Leisure Library Series for 1887.

8. HYGIENIC THERAPEUTICS. This work, which treats of Massage, Exercise, Hydrotherapy, Aerotherapy and Climatotherapy, has been published in its entirety in the columns of the Therapeutic Gazette, 1887–1888.

From the above statement, it will be seen that all of the *Leçons de Clinique Thérapeutique*, a work which has had no little popularity and success in France, has now been rendered into English, except Vol. II, which is devoted to the treatment of Diseases of the Liver Kidneys and Lungs.

The present volume comprises Diseases of the Liver, and the succeeding volume on Diseases of the Kidneys, will leave only about half of Vol. II of the *Leçons* untranslated.

I hardly need to apologize for the omission of many pages of the bibliographical indications. Some abridgement was deemed necessary, and it seemed that these references, pertaining, for the most part, to works in foreign languages, might better be spared than any other part

It is unnecessary that I should call attention to the practical character of this work, and the wealth of research which it embodies, or allude to the prominent position which Dujardin-Beaumetz now occupies in the estimation of his colleagues in the medical profession everywhere, as a leader in therapeutics.

TRANSLATOR.

NEWBURYPORT, MASS., July 1st, 1888.

TABLE OF CONTENTS.

CHAPTER I.

The Liver from a Therapeutic Standpoint.

SUMMARY.—General Considerations on the Liver—Anatomy of the Liver—The Hepatic Lobule—The Interlobular Spaces—The Physiology of the Liver—The Liver as a Glycogenic Organ—The Liver as a Producer of Urea—Accumulation of Medicinal Substances—Destruction of Alkaloids by the Liver—Difference of Action of Medicines according as Introduced by the Mouth or the Skin—Accumulation of Doses—The Liver as the Organ of the Biliary Secretion Cholesterine—Bile Pigment—The Biliary Salts—Secretion of Bile—Action of the Nervous System on this Secretion....

CHAPTER II.

Cholagogues.

SUMMARY:—Cholagogue Medicaments—Physiological Experiments on Cholagogues—Process of Rohrig—Process of Rutherford and Vignal—Cholagogue Purgatives—Cholagogue Action of Calomel—New Cholagogues of Vegetable Origin — Euonymin — Iridin—

CHAPTER III.

Treatment of Biliary Lithiasis.

CHAPTER IV.

Treatment of Jaundice.

CHAPTER V.

Treatment of Engorgements of the Liver.

CHAPTER VI.

Treatment of Inflammations of the Liver.

XII

CHAPTER VII.

Treatment of Hydatid Cysts of the Liver.

CHAPTER I.

THE LIVER FROM A THERAPEUTIC STANDPOINT.

SUMMARY.—General Considerations on the Liver—Anatomy of the Liver—The Hepatic Lobule—The Interlobular Spaces The Physiology of the Liver—The Liver as a Glycogenic Organ—The Liver as a Producer of Urea—Accumulation of Medicinal Substances—Destruction of Alkaloids by the Liver—Difference of Action of Medicines according as introduced by the Mouth or the Skin—Accumulation of Doses—The Liver as the Organ of the Biliary Secretion Cholesterine—Bile Pigment—The Biliary Salts—Secretion of Bile—Action of the Nervous System on this Secretion.

GENTLEMEN:—I intend to devote the present course of lectures to the therapeutics of diseases of the liver and kidneys, diseases which are frequent and often demand active treatment. I will begin with the study of affections of the liver, but before entering upon the main part of my subject, I desire to set forth in this lecture certain general considerations on the liver from a therapeutic point of view.

You know the importance which I place on an exact knowledge of the anatomy and physiology of the organ whose diseased condition claims your intervention; such knowledge is the indispensable basis of a rational and scientific treatment; I will therefore sum up briefly what we know respecting this organ.

2 x

I shall be brief on the anatomy of the liver, as you are already familiar with this subject through the works of Kiernan, Hering, and especially of Prof. Charcot. You know the ordinary description of the hepatic lobule, which Kiernan has compared to an oak-leaf, whose petiole and mid rib represent the interlobular vein, while the lateral branches, formed by vessels and cellular tissue, constitute a frame work in which are lodged the hepatic cells discovered by Purkinje and Henle.* You also know the regular, almost geometric, disposition of the hepatic cells, and the constitution of these cells, which contain pigmentary granulations, and nuclei with roundish nucleoli.

---

* The hepatic lobule is constituted by a group of cells around which are blood vessels, bile ducts, lymphatic lacunæ, and connective tissue fibrillæ. Grouped together, these cells form little five or six faced prismatic masses, whose base rests on branches of the hepatic vein (sub-lobular vein). In the centre of the lobule is seen a small vein (intra-lobular vein); each lobule is enveloped by a sheath from the capsule of Glisson which supports the ramifications of the vena portae (interlobular veins), which, according to Hering's comparison, unite in the interlobular spaces after the manner of a tree which plunges its roots into the interstices of a rocky soil; these veins are accompanied by arterioles from the hepatic artery, bile ducts and lymphatics.

The hepatic cell has an average diameter of from 16–19 μ (Kölliker), (Henle and Kölliker); it has one or more nuclei of 9 μ in diameter, which are provided with a nucleolus. Some of the cells have even as many as from three to five nuclei (Henle). The contents of the cells consist, 1st, of pigmentary

The web which contains the cells is constituted by a connective tissue framework, which, when affected by hyperplasia, gives rise to true cirrhosis; then by blood vessels, lymphatics and bile ducts, forming a multiple capillary net-work surrounding each of the cells.

I must call your attention to the interlobular spaces, upon which Kiernan has rightly placed so much stress, and which Sabourin, in his researches on the constitution of the hepatic gland, has considered as the biliary lobule.*

These spaces are, in fact, the seat and starting point of abscesses, of tubercles, of syphilomata and of lymphomata of the liver. Alcoholic cirrhosis, a disease which you see so frequently in our wards, and to

---

granulations; 2d, of granules with pale borders, which have not the reaction of fat and which mostly fill the cell; 3d, granules with dark borders, shiny, giving with ether and osmic acid the reaction of fat. Charcot, to whom we are indebted for these notions respecting the cell, remarks that these fat granules are to a certain extent found in the animal and in man in a multitude of physicial conditions, such as lactation and digestion.

* The interlobular spaces are formed by the polygonal space which several lobules leave between them; they contain branches of the portal vein and hepatic artery, bile ducts, and lymphatics; all send ramifications between the neighboring lobules, and all the elements are surrounded by Glisson's capsule. This is according to Kiernan's description. Sabourin has since modified slightly the anatomical and,

which I shall return when the subject of its treatment comes up, has for origin these same spaces, being due to a perivascular inflammation affecting the ramifications of the vena portæ, as has been well shown by the researches of Solowief and Charcot.

If the anatomy of the liver has made manifest progress the past few years, and seems to-day almost complete, it is necessary to bear in mind that the knowledge of the physiology of this organ has not kept pace with that of the anatomy, and there are still certain functions of the liver concerning which physiologists are not completely agreed.

Nothing, perhaps, in the history of medicine is more interesting than a general survey of the endeavors which have been made to find out the functions of the liver.

For centuries the world accepted with unquestioning faith the doctrine of Galen, who taught that the hepatic gland was the centre of animal heat and the organ which presided over sanguification. Then came the discovery of the bile in the 17th century, and

---

so to speak, classical conception of the liver. He considers the hepatic gland as constituted by tubular elements. He takes, as the centre of the biliary lobule, the portal interspace, into which abut the pyramidal segments formed by the hepatic lobules just as they have been heretofore described. This aggregate constitutes a glandular territory, perfectly limited, to which he gives the name of biliary lobule. (Sabourin, Soc. de Biol., 17 December, 1881).

all the old doctrines were lost sight of, and the liver was reduced to the simple office of an emunctory, designed to separate from the economy an excrementitious liquid, the bile. But modern experimental physiology was destined to restore to the organ the high functions which were assigned to it by Galen and his school. In fact, it is, as you know, in the liver, in the hepatic cell itself, that Claude Bernard places the glycogenic function. The same organ also, according to Murchison, Brouardel, and Charcot, is the seat of that physiological process which is the most manifest expression of the combustions of the economy, namely, the production of urea. Lastly, a great number of physiologists are of accord in affirming the hæmatopoietic functions of this gland.

As you see, the liver has regained in our day its former high importance.

From a therapeutic point of view, the study of the functions of the liver is, it must be admitted, much more limited ; we have really observed only the action of certain substances on the biliary secretion, and are ignorant of the action of medicaments on the liver as a glycogenic organ.

As for the liver considered as a producer of urea, physiologists are far from being fully agreed. To the labors of Murchison and of Brouardel have been opposed other experiments and other researches, and in particular those of De Sinety and Martin, which go to show that perhaps too much has been affirmed as to the relation of the liver to urea-formation, and that this excrementitious principle has not for its exclusive seat of production the hepatic gland, but that it is formed in all the glands and all the tissues of the economy.

De Sinety has observed that in frogs, which survive for some time the total ablation of the liver, the urine continues to contain urea.

This doctrine of the formation of urea in the liver is one of the most contested in physiology; two orders of proofs have been alleged in substantiation, physiological and pathological.

(a). Meissner, Kuhn, Lehmann, have shown that while the muscles contain no urea, the liver contains notable quantities.

Cyon has shown, moreover, that in 100 cubic centimeters of blood which has not yet passed through the liver, there exists 0.09 of urea, while there is present 0.14 of urea in the same blood after haviug traversed that organ.

Gathgens and Hensius have maintained that albuminous matters in the liver break up into glycogen and urea.

(b). From a pathological point of view, Murchison, Charcot, Brouardel have seen that in diseases of the liver, which destroy more or less completely this organ, the quantity of urea notably diminishes. Hence Brouardel has concluded that the quantity of urea formed and eliminated in the 24 hours is dependent on two principal influences:

1. The state of integrity or alteration of the hepatic cells;
2. The greater or less activity of the hepatic circulation.

Murchison has gone even farther, and maintained that the liver even fabricates uric acid. But to these facts have been objected other experiments and other analyses, and in particular those of De Sinety and Martin before alluded to, which tend to invalidate this teaching. Physiologists have laid stress upon the preponderant rôle of alimentation, as the quantity of urea varies according to the food ingested; and the more probable view would seem to be that urea is not formed exclusively in the liver, but throughout the entire organism.

But there is one point in this study which ought to detain us longer: I allude to the passage of medicinal substances through the liver after having been introduced by the digestive tube, and their more or less prolonged sojourn in this gland. This is one of the most interesting subjects connected with the physiology of the liver, and you will see that by virtue of the experiments of Lussana, Heger, Schiff and Jacques, we may derive therefrom fruitful therapeutic results.

You are aware that for a long time physiologists have known the possibility of the accumulation of certain toxic substances in the liver, and it is a rule in legal medicine in cases of poisoning to analyze the liver, in order to find there traces of arsenic, copper, lead and other substances which have been suspected of determining symptoms of poisoning.

Paganuzzi, of Padua, was the first to show the difference which exists in the mode of elimination when certain salts of iron are introduced by the veins of the general circulation, and when they are introduced by the mesenteric veins; in the first case the salt is eliminated by the kidneys, in the second by the bile.*

---

* Annuschat has made some interesting experiments on the elimination of lead by the bile in lead poisoning. He has

Lussana, basing himself on some previous experiments of Schiff, since verified by Rosenkranz, researches which have shown that the bile secreted in the intestine returns to the liver to be eliminated anew, verified the experiment of Paganuzzi, and affirmed as the result thereof that the reconstituent and hæmatopoietic effects of ferruginous preparations are due to the intimate action on the hepatic cells of the salts of iron, which, when introduced by the digestive tube into the liver, are then eliminated by the bile and pass back again into the liver by the entero-hepatic circulation described by Schiff.

In 1873, Hegar, of Brussels, applying to the elucidation of this question Ludwig's ingenious method of artificial circulations effected in isolated organs, discovered that when blood containing a large dose of nicotine is made to pass through the hepatic gland, this alkaloid disappears completely in the liver, so that you no longer find any trace of it in the hepatic veins.

In 1877, Schiff discovered that not only does nicotine in passing through the liver lose its toxic properties, but that other alkaloids are almost as completely destroyed by this gland, and he mentions among the latter hyoscyamin.

Lastly, in 1880, Victor Jacques, a Belgian physician, completed these researches by showing that a

shown that in animals the greater the ingestion of lead the more abundant its elimination by the bile, and that the lead in he intestine comes in large part from the biliary secretion.

certain number of alkaloids introduced by the digestive passage sojourn a while in the liver, and that
some are in part destroyed in the hepatic gland, and
that others may be eliminated after a limited time,
whether by the bile or lymphatics.

What is the intimate action of these substances
on the hepatic cell? Are more or less stable com-
binations formed with these alkaloids, which either
destroy the properties of the latter, or which, being
slowly dissociated by an excess of albumen, are
thereupon eliminated anew? We do not know, but it
is none the less certain that these researches enable
us to explain facts heretofore very obscure.

Among these facts is the marked difference which
exists between the effects of medicaments, and in particular of alkaloids, when introduced by the mouth
and when administered by the hypodermic method.
The prompt and energetic action of subcutaneous injections finds an easy explanation. The medicine
passes immediately into the general circulation, and
brings its therapeutic or toxic action to bear upon
different parts of the economy. When introduced by
the mouth, however, the alkaloid passes into the liver,
and there it is in part destroyed or tardily eliminated
by the hepatic gland, hence we see the superior advantage of hypodermic injections, which render every
day such marked service; and we can never be too
grateful to Wood, of England, and to my very regretted
Master, Behier, for having introduced and popularized
this method.

This complete destruction or tardy elimination of alkaloids by the hepatic gland gives us a physiological explanation of two other orders of facts: (1) the innocuousness of certain poisons introduced by the mouth, such as curare, of which Claude Bernard has shown the absolute inefficacy when absorbed by the alimentary canal, and (2) phenomenon so frequently observed when certain alkaloids are given by the mouth, and in particular the alkaloids of the solanaceæ—I refer to the tardy effect of these alkaloids, and what Gubler has described under the name of "accumulation of doses."

You are acquainted with all these facts; you know that when we give atropine or duboisin in very minute doses, and for several days in succession, we are in danger of seeing symptoms of poisoning set in, although the daily dose remains the same. To-day, by virtue of the experiments which I have just mentioned, we have a clear and scientific explanation of these facts. The alkaloid is absorbed by the digestive tube and fixes itself in the liver. Then, at a variable time, it is eliminated into the intestine with the bile, or passes into the circulation with the lymphatics, and its presence goes to augment the portion which is absorbed into the general circulation of the daily doses which you have administered.

Permit me to add a word: I have just told you that medicaments introduced under the skin and passing directly into the general circulation are eliminated by the kidneys. I shall show you, as we go on, that if this elimination is wanting, the therapeutic effects of the alkaloid cease, and give place to toxic symptoms.

It would be important to study, as opportunity may occur, the influence of diseases of the liver, and in particular of those which completely destroy the hepatic cell such as cirrhosis, on the action of alkaloids introduced by the mouth. Here there is an important series of researches to be made, to which I invite your attention.

But this action of the hepatic gland does not pertain exclusively to the vegetable alkaloids, but also, and equally, to the toxic alkaloids which we have seen to be incessantly produced in the economy.

In my work on Diseases of the Stomach and Intestines, I showed you the important part which these ptomaines or leucomaines play in the economy, and I dwelt on their elimination by the different emunctories.

The liver has an important function in the elimination and destruction of these toxic products. Hence, when its parenchyma is altered, you can understand how these toxic substances may accumulate in the blood and produce their deleterious effects, effects which play a preponderant rôle in the symptoms which accompany destruction of the hepatic gland.

This discovery of the morbid poisons which the economy produces during life, and the important part which the liver plays in such cases, justifies somewhat the view set forth by Lautenbach* several years ago.

The liver is the organ that secretes the bile, and from this point of view it possesses for us a great therapeutic interest, for there are numerous substances which modify the biliary secretion; these are called cholagogues. But before setting forth the physiological experiments which demonstrate this action, I shall make a few remarks concerning the bile and its secretion in the normal state.

Considered in the most general manner, bile is constituted of three elements, cholesterine, bile pigment, biliary acids and salts.†

Cholesterine, which the researches of Berthelot

---

*Lautenbach basing himself on the experiments of Schiff, maintained that the liver not only destroys poisons introduced into the economy but that the organism in the physiological stage produces a poison which is destroyed by the liver as fast as it is generated. (Phil'a Med. Times, May 20, 1887.)

† According to Charles Robin the composition of the bile is as follows:

Water, 915.90—819.90	Glycocholate or Cholate of Sodium, traces.
Chloride of Sodium, 2.77 to 3.50	
Phosphate of Lime, 1.00 to 2.50	Leucin, Tyrosin, Urea, traces.
" " Potassium, 0.75 to 1.50	Cholesterine, 1.60 to 2.66
" " Lime, 0.50 to 1.35	Lecithin,
" " Magnesia, 0.45 to 0.80	Margarin, Olein and } 3.20 to 31.00
Salts of Iron, 0.15 to 0.30	traces of Fat,
" Magnesia, traces to 0.12	Biliverdin, 14.00 to 30.00
Silica, 0.30 to 0.66	Mucosin, traces.
Taurocholate of Sodium, 56.50 to 106.60	

have caused to be classed among the monatomic alcohols, is a fatty substance which presents itself to the
microscope under the form of rhomboidal tablets.
You know also that these crystals have a characteristic
reaction which consists in the red coloration which
they assume in contact with sulphuric acid. To-day
everyone is agreed in adopting the theory of Flint as
to the origin of this substance, and Vulpian in his remarkable " Lessons on the Bile " has accepted this
view which regards cholesterine as a product of disassimilation of the nervous substance. Feltz and
Ritter have shown, on the other hand, that this substance when it accumulates in the blood does not produce any grave toxic symptoms.*

Trefanowski has attained similar results, finding in a
thousand parts of bile from the gall bladder of a human subject, 908.70 of water, 91.22 of fixed matters, of which 28.56
were glycocholates and taurocholates.

* Cholesterine ($C_{26} H_{44} O + H_2 O$) discovered by Poullet
and De la Salle in biliary calculi then by Fourcroy in a
desiccated liver, was studied by Chevreul in 1824, who gave it
the name which it bears to-day. It is a non-saponifiable fat,
white, crystallizable, insoluble in water, soluble in soap and
water, ether, wood spirit, boiling alcohol, glacial acetic acid,
and in solutions of taurocholic acid and taurocholates; it contains almost eighty-four per cent. of carbon and twelve per
cent. of hydrogen; the crystals present themselves under the
form of rhomboidal plates, which are thin and brilliant and
fuse at 140° C.

Cholesterine is met in divers regions of the organism,

As for the bile pigment, bilirubin, it is an azotized non-albuminous principle derived from the decomposition of the coloring matters of the globules, whose properties Tarchanoff and Vossius have thoroughly studied; in fact, from a chemical point of view, there is a great similarity between hæmatin and bilirubin, and you will see when we come to take up the subject of jaundice that the possible transformation of the former into the latter has given a name to a special form of jaundice, hæmatogenous jaundice (icterus sanguinis). We shall see, also, that bilirubin has a characteristic reaction, and that the most important and best known is that determined by nitrous nitric acid, which in contact with bilirubin gives a play of colors; red, green, blue, yellow and brown.*

---

and in the blood; it is very abundant in the nervous centres, existing in greatest quantity in the white substance.

Since the researches of Austin Flint, 1868 ("Experimental Researches on a New Function of the Liver"), the majority of physiologists have regarded cholesterine as a product of disassimilation eliminated by the liver and passing into the intestine with the bile. Beneke stands alone in regarding it as a product of the hepatic secretion contributing to the resorption of the fats in the intestine.

*Bilirubin, an azotized non-albuminous principle, presents itself under the form of a red amorphous powder, or of needle-shaped crystals; it is held in solution by the biliary acids.

There are two tests in common use: Gmelin's and Schwanda's. Gmelin's test, which is also the common test for

But the truly essential part of the bile consists in the biliary salts, glycocholates and taurocholates of sodium. You know that these two acids easily break up, the one into cholic and cholalic acids, the other into taurin and glycocol. Pettenkoffer has given a means of readily detecting these acids. If you subject them to contact with a mixture of sulphuric acid and sugar, you see them take on a beautiful violet purple color.

These acids give their principal character to the

-----

hæmatoidin, is the nitrous nitric acid, which, instilled drop by drop into a solution containing bilirubin, gives a play of colors; green, blue, violet, red and brown. When hæmatoidin predominates, the violet color is the most pronounced, while the green color is the most marked when bilirubin predominates. Schwanda's test is acetic acid, which when heated with bilirubin, gives a green color.

Bilirubin and hæmatoidin are very much alike; they differ principally in this respect, that in hæmatoidin an atom of iron replaces the two atoms of hydrogen which exist in the molecule of bilirubin. There are other biliary pigments which seem to be derivatives of bilirubin, such as biliverdin, bilifulvin, bilifuscin, biliprasin and bilihomin. Studeler has given to bilirubin the formula: $C_{16} H_{18} NO_3$. He regards biliverdin as bilirubin plus water and oxygen.

Vossius has made some recent experiments on the biliary secretion, and on the quantity of coloring matters secreted in 24 hours. He has shown that in a dog weighing 25 kilogrammes, the quantity of bile varies from 60 to 150 cubic centimetres in 12 hours, and that the coloring matter of the bile varies between 0.0487 and 0.056; the average furnished by

biliary secretion, and in fact, while we have seen that
cholesterine originates in processes of disassimilation
of the cerebro-spinal axis, and the coloring matter of
the bile has for its origin the hæmatin of the blood
globules, the biliary salts are formed solely in the
liver, and are a product of the secretion of this gland.
This is, you must remember, a fact of capital importance, which clearly differentiates the kidney from the
liver, and while the one does nothing but separate
from the economy substances which have accumulated
in the blood, the other produces from elements in the
blood special substances which are characteristic of

---

eight experiments was 0.056. This richness in coloring matters is little modified by food; it nevertheless augments when
the animal is subjected to a regimen exclusively hydro-carbon-
aceous. When considerable quantities of hæmoglobin are injected into the blood, the coloring matter of the bile is not augmented. On the other hand, when you inject distilled water
into the veins, or a 5 per cent. solution of sodium chloride,
you augment in a notable manner the coloring matter, and the
same thing takes place when you introduce coloring matter into
the blood. This shows, as Tarchanoff has pointed out, that
the liver has the property of separating from the blood the coloring matter of the bile, to incorporate it with its proper
secretion.

To test the coloring matter in the urine, Rosenbach proposes the following process: The urine is passed through
white filtering paper, and when the filter is dry, a drop of nitric
acid is let fall upon it, and then several concentric zones show
themselves; green, blue, violet and yellow.

The glycocholates and taurocholates of soda are obtained

its secretion. The experiments of Muller, Lehmann, Kund, and especially the beautiful experiment of Molesschott, who performed ablation of the liver in frogs, and did not find the biliary acids to accumulate in the blood, are absolutely demonstrative on this point.

Where is the bile elaborated? Must we admit, as Charles Robin suggests, that it is in the glands of

---

under a crystalline form. They form from 55 to 61 per cent. of the solid residue of the bile.

Their acids are glycocholic or cholic acid discovered in 1825 by Tiedmann and Gmelin, and taurocholic or cholalic acid.

Glychocolic acid ($C_{16} H_{18} NO_6$) is but little soluble in water and ether, more soluble in alcohol. It is obtained under the form of fine needles. Under the influence of hydrochloric acid it breaks up into cholalic acid and glycocol (sugar of gelatin).

Cholalic acid, obtained for the first time by Demarquay, presents itself in the amorphous state or in four-sided prisms with bevelled edges. By the action of prolonged heat it is converted into dyslysin. Moreover, dilute sulphuric or hydrochloric acid transform it at first into choloidic acid, then into dyslysin.

Taurocholic acid ($C_{26} H_{46} NO_4 S$) has not yet been obtained in a crystalline state. Under the influence of heat and of caustic alkalies, it breaks up into cholalic acid and into taurin.

Taurin, discovered by Gmelin, crystallizes in 4 or 6 sided prisms, terminated by pyramids with four facets. It contains sulphur in considerable proportions. Like glycocholic acid, taurocholic acid exercises a right handed polarization.

3 ⟩

the bile ducts that the secretion of the biliary acids takes place, while to the hepatic cell is reserved the glycogenic function? Must we locate in the hepatic cell itself this secretion? This is a question which the researches of Kolliker seem to have solved, for he found the biliary acids in the hepatic cells. It is, then, in the cell that the secretion of bile takes place, and it remains for us to study what are the influences which cause this secretion to vary.

In the physiological state, the bile, as Colin has shown, flows continuously into the intestine, but this flow is subject to intermittences; for example, during the period of digestion, and under the influences of certain emotions, the secretion is much augmented. We shall study more at length the various modifications in the biliary secretion in a future lecture devoted to biliary lithiasis.

The quantity of bile secreted in twenty-four hours in a dog weighing ten kilogrammes is 150 grammes (Nasse and Plater). In the cat, according to Stackman, the quantity secreted per kilogramme of the weight of the animal is sixteen grammes in the twenty-four hours.

This proportion is the same as that found by Scott & Ritter; thus a man of average weight, say 150 pounds, will secrete one kilogramme, or about two pounds of bile in twenty-four hours.

This figure is, however, higher than that furnished by direct experiments on patients with biliary fistulæ.

De Witch and Westphalen, in two cases of the kind, the one a man, the other a woman, noted that the quantity of bile secreted in twenty-four hours was about 500 grammes.

You know that when we tie the hepatic artery, we do not cause the secretion of bile to cease. It is the same when the ligature embraces the portal vein, leaving the artery intact. What do such experiments show? They prove this, that owing to the numerous anastomoses, it suffices that the hepatic shall be supplied with blood, it matters not from what source, in order to accomplish its function of secretion.

This is so true, that when you bleed animals, you see the secretion of bile notably diminish; on the other hand, if you make an intra-venous injection of water, the biliary secretion is augmented.

But there is a physiological process which notably augments this secretion, viz.: digestion, or, more strictly speaking, the irritation produced by food or chyme on the intestinal mucosa. There is in these cases a double action: first, an augmentation in the production of bile, then augmentation of the excretion caused by increase of the contractile movements, of which the gall bladder and its ducts are the seat.

In this regard, there is a fact noticed by Röhrig and Vulpian which presents a great interest, viz.: that when you inject water into the intestine of animals under experimentation, you see the secretion of the bile augment.*

---

* Numerous experimenters have investigated the mode of secretion of bile. Malpighi, Schiff, and others, found that after ligature of the hepatic artery, the biliary secretion still went on. Oré, of Bordeaux, by numerous experiments on

As for the influence of the nervous system on this secretion, it is not at all doubtful; at the same time, experiments in this direction are not very decisive. Certainly, the vaso-motor nerves—vaso-constrictors and vaso-dilators—undergo there, as everywhere else, modifications from reflex influence, but, as I have said before, we need more light on this subject.

Such, gentlemen, are the brief considerations which I wished to present respecting the liver and its

---

cats and dogs, also noticed that the secretion continued after obliteration of the vena portæ, on condition, however, that the obliteration was not made suddenly. Schiff undertook several series of researches. In a first series he tied the branches of the cœliac axis and the inferior diaphragmatic artery. In a second series of experiments, he tied the portal vein and the small branches going to the liver; he separated the hepatic artery and tied in one mass the hepatico-duodenal ligament and the common bile duct; the animals died in convulsions an hour and a half after the operation. Finally, in his third series of experiments Schiff gradually interrupted the circulation of the portal vein, and observed that the biliary secretion persisted.

To explain this fact, Schiff says that the secretion continues by reason of persistence of the portal circulation, due to the accessory para-umbilical portal veins.

With regard to the influence of the nervous system on the biliary secretion, numerous experiments have been made by Heidenhain, Röhrig, Munk and others.

Heidenhain in operating on dogs, has shown that electrization of the spinal cord produces, first, an augmentation then retardation, in the secretion of bile. He thinks that the retardation of the flow of bile is a consequence of the con-

functions. Now that we know the general particulars of its anatomy and physiology, and the conditions which preside over the secretion of the bile, we can study the action of certain substances on this secretion, and pass in review that important group of medicaments which have so important a part in the treatment of diseases of the liver; I refer to cholagogues, which will be the subject of my next lecture.

---

striction of the vessels and diminution of the blood pressure in the interior of the liver. The acceleration of the flow of bile, on the contrary, is to be attributed to contraction of the bile ducts. Munk has arrived at the same conclusions as Heidenhain. As for Rohrig, he has also observed the augmentation of the biliary secretion under electrization of the cord. But electrization of the central end of the sciatic nerve does not, he says. produce this augmentation of the secretion, as Heidenhain and Monk have affirmed.

Vulpian, moreover, remarked that section of the pneumogastrics and experimental lesions of the floor of the fourth ventricle produce a congestion of the liver with increased activity of the biliary secretion. These facts have, he thinks, a high importance. They explain the mechanism of the jaundice resulting from strong mental emotions, such as fear, anger, etc.

CHAPTER II.

CHOLAGOGUES.

SUMMARY:—Cholagogue Medicaments—Physiological Experiments on Cholagogues—Process of Rohrig—Process of Rutherford and Vignal—Cholagogue Purgatives—Cholagogue Action of Calomel—New Cholagogues of Vegetable Origin—Euonymin—Iridin—Baptisin—Hydrastin—Juglandin—Sanguinarin—Phytolaccin—Cholagogues of Mineral Origin—On the Action of Alkalies as Cholagogues.

GENTLEMEN:—When I was lecturing on purgatives, I told you that there were certain of them which act by augmenting the secretion of bile. It is to this group that the name of cholagogues has been given. I told you, also, that I was intending to study more at length this class of purgatives when I came to diseases of the liver, and the subject properly comes up for consideration to day. But before enumerating the different substances which enter into this group, I will first examine upon what experimental bases the study of cholagogues rests.

Formerly it was by examination of the stools that physicians were enabled to classify these medicaments, and according as the stools were more or less bilious, the medicine was considered as having a greater or less action on the liver and was reckoned cholagogue. This method, which was not a very scientific one, has given place to more precise researches, for which we are principally indebted to certain foreign physicians.*

In 1863 Hanfield Jones was the first to enter on this experimental method. He gave certain medicinal substances to animals which he afterwards killed, and he then examined the state of the liver and intestines; according as he found the hepatic gland more or less congested, he concluded that the medicament had a more or less energetic action on the biliary secretion. This it must be admitted, was a somewhat rude and primitive process, which had been nevertheless put in usage by previous experimenters and in particular by Pecholier† in studying the action of calomel.

In 1867 and '68, the British Association, which has done so much to elucidate important problems in therapeutics, and in particular, that of the action of alexipharmic medicines and of antagonism in therapeutics, submitted the question of cholagogues for discussion, and appointed a commission consisting of Arthur Gamgee and Hughes Bennett to undertake a series of experiments to ascertain the action of the so-called cholagogues.

This commission made an important report, based

---

* Arthur Gamger, Rutherford, Hughes Bennett, Rohrig, etc.

† Pecholier ("Indications for the Employment of Calomel in the Treatment of Dysentery") noticed in 1865 that in hares to which he had administered calomel, the liver was very much congested.

on numerous experiments performed upon dogs,
which were all put on the same diet and subjected to
the action of certain medicaments whose influence on
the biliary secretion was then studied by careful analysis.

In 1873, Röhrig, in Germany, completed and perfected this mode of research.

He curarized dogs and subjected them to artificial
respiration. Then, after taking care to empty the gall
bladder and tie the cystic duct, he introduced into
the extremity of the common bile duct a tube ending
in a tapering point, like a dropping tube; then, by the
aid of a metronome beating seconds, he counted the
number of drops of bile flowing in a given time by the
tube, and thus studied the action of different substances introduced into the stomach or digestive tube
of animals under experimentation.

You see that quite an improvement was effected
in the way of scientific definiteness, as indicated by the
distance which separtes the method of Jones from
that of Röhrig; but progress did not stop here.

Rutherford and Vignal, in 1875, repeated and
improved the processes of Röhrig; they proceeded at
first as did the latter experimenter, that is to say, they
curarized the animal, emptied the gall bladder, and
applied a ligature to the cystic duct but instead of introducing into the common bile duct a simple tapering
tube, they employed a glass pipette adapted to a rubber
tube, terminated at its distal extremity by another

glass tube dipping into a graduated test measure; then they calculated the quantity of bile secreted in a given space of time.

In some preliminary researches, these experiments proved first of all that curare has no action on the biliary secretion, and that during the entire duration of the experiment the bile kept its composition almost unchanged; then they showed that in the normal state in the dog the quantity of bile secreted is about 20 cu. c. m. per kilogramme of the weight of the body and per hour, and it is by relying on this latter figure that they established the coefficient of cholagogue medicaments. This word *coefficient*, then, indicates the quantity of bile secreted in an hour and corresponding to 1 kilogramme of the weight of the animal; the more that figure exceeds the sum of 20 cu. c. m., the greater the action of the medicament on the biliary secretion. Note in this connection that the substance under experimentation was not introduced by the mouth, but inserted into the duodenum; it is in this way that Rutherford and Vignal have arrived at the following table which I here place before you:

COEFFICIENTS EXPRESSING THE ABSOLUTE QUANTITY OF BILE
OBTAINED IN EACH EXPERIMENT DURING ONE HOUR
PER KILOGRAMME OF THE WEIGHT OF THE
ANIMAL.

Podophyllin (with addition of bile)	0.01	Phosphate of sodium	0.44
Aloes	0.93	Sanguinarin	0.40
Salicylate of sodium	0.89	Nitro-hydrochloric acid,	0.39
Corrosive sublimate	0.85	Baptisin	0.39
Extract of physostigma,	0.75	Ipecac	0.38
Corrosive sublimate	0.72	Hydrastin	0.38
Aloes (without bile)	0.69	Sulphate of sodium	0.38
Salicylate of sodium	0.66	Extract of physostigma,	0.36
Benzoate of sodium	0.64	Jalap	0.35
Iridin	0.63	Rochelle salt	0.33
Salicylate of sodium	0.56	Rhubarb	0.32
Corrosive sublimate	0.55	Hydrastin	0.32
Ipecacuanha	0.55	Juglandine	0.32
Benzoate of ammonia	0.54	Leptandrin	0.31
Podophyllin(without bile)	0.47	Sanguinarin	0.30
Euonymin (with bile)	0.47	Jalap	0.29
Corrosive sublimate	0.47	Baptisin	0.29
Phytolaccin	0.47	Phytolaccin	0.29
Sulphate of potassium	0.47	Hydrastin	0.28
Sanguinarin	0.46	Colocynth	0.27
Euonymin	0.46	Leptandrin	0 27
Colocynth	0.45	Sulphate of sodium	0.25
Colchicum	0.45	Colchicum	0.20

You will notice, first of all, the change which has
been effected by these experimental researches in the
old group of cholagogues, constituted by podophyllin,

aloes, rhubarb and senna. This group has in great part well stood the test of experimentation; podophyllin still holds in the tables of some of the experimenters the very first place among the cholagogues.*

But the action of podophyllin is characterized by this curious fact, to which I shall again allude, viz., that its maximum effect, as far as the activity of the biliary secretion is concerned, does not take place with large, but with moderate doses. Aloes and rhubarb remain still good cholagogues, while the drastics properly so-called, colocynth, scammony and croton oil are very moderate cholagogues.

Thus far, you see, experimentation has done complete justice to the medicaments called cholagogues, but this is not the case when we take up the study of calomel, and we have here, it must be confessed, one

---

* The experiments of Röhrig, on the one hand, and of Rutherford and Vignal on the other, do not agree respecting the action of these cholagogues on the biliary secretion, as may be seen by the following classification:

CHOLAGOGUES IN THEIR ORDER OF EXCELLENCE.	CHOLAGOGUES IN THEIR ORDER OF EXCELLENCE.
According to Röhrig:	According to Rutherford and Vignal:
Colocynth,	Podophyllin.
Jalap,	Rhubarb,
Aloes,	Aloes,
Senna,	Colchicum,
Rhubarb.	Senna.

of the most delicate and difficult points connected with the question, and one which shows how difficult it often is to bring into harmony physiological experimenters and clinicians.

From the time of Paracelsus and Von Helmont down to our days, physicians have vaunted the action of calomel on the liver; the green stools produced by this medicament were considered an undoubted sign of the elective action of calomel on the hepatic gland; and whatever Stillé may have said to the contrary, who affirmed that the color of the stools produced by calomel were due to a subsulphuret of mercury, it is to-day demonstrated by the experiments of Golding Bird and Simon, and especially by the researches of Michèa, that this coloration is due to a biliary pigment.

If clinical experience is unanimous in affirming the cholagogue action of calomel, quite as decided agreement and unanimity exist among experimental physiologists in denying this action. Consult the experiments of Scott, Mosler, Kölliker, Müller, of Bennet, of Rohrig and of Rutherford, and all will tell you that calomel does not augment the secretion of bile in the dog but that it diminishes it.

How are we going to reconcile results so contradictory. Some authorities, and in particular Fraser, have attempted an explanation; the experimenters, they say, put themselves in special conditions which were different from what one observes in the man whether well or sick. Between the curarized dog living by artificial respiration and the man, there is a great difference. But this argument seems to me to miss the point, and for this reason: if it were sound we ought to reject *in toto* all the experiments on cholagogues. for the same objection applies to all the experiments, which would thereby be hopelessly vitiated. But this none of the authorities are willing to grant, and there is general agreement that the results of the experiments as far as most of the medicaments are concerned are trustworthy, and valid.

Murchison seems nearer the truth when he says that mercury augments the biliary excretion without augmenting the secretion; *i. e.* by exciting the contractions of the bile ducts, by diminishing the catarrhal congestion of these ducts, by modifying perhaps the bile itself, calomel causes a greater quantity of bile to flow into the intestine without, however, augmenting the secretion of this liquid.

I am inclined to take the same view of the case as Murchison, and, while giving the precedence to clinical experience over physiological experimentation, I persist in regarding calomel as one of the best cholagogues; but I would associate with it another mercurial preparation, which some have supposed to be void of cholagogue properties, namely, corrosive sublimate. In fact, while the mild chloride of mercury, when administered experimentally, diminishes rather than augments the biliary secretion, the corrosive chloride, on the contrary, according to Rutherford, augments this secretion; therefore, I advise you, when you wish to obtain the full benefit of the salts of mercury in the treatment of hepatic affections, to combine calomel with corrosive sublimate, and to prescribe pills containing ten centigrams of calomel and two milligrams of the sublimate. These pills, in the dose of one or two at bedtime, have a marked cholagogue effect.

As you see, the group of cholagogues, with the exception of calomel, passes, as it were, intact through the hands of the experimenters. To this group should be joined ipecac, whose particular action on the liver you have already learned theoretically. For you cannot have forgotten what I said while on the treatment of dysentery, when I endeavored to explain the heroic curative action of this medicament by the excitation which it produces on the biliary secretion. This view is confirmed by experimentation, and you see by the work of Rutherford that ipecac deserves a place among the best cholagogues.

But the researches of the English experimenters have not had merely for result to confirm what tradition had taught us concerning the cholagogues, but also to call attention to a new group of medicaments of whose action on the biliary secretion we were absolutely ignorant. These are certain new medicaments which I am going to pass in review, and which I shall classify under two heads; those derived from the vegetable kingdom and those from the mineral.

The first of these groups, by far the most important, is composed of a series of substances called by the English writers baptisin, euonymin, hydrastin, iridin, juglandin, leptandrin, phytolaccin. These are aqueous or hydro-alcoholic extracts of uncertain chemical composition, and which, if they are to take a place in therapeutics, need to be studied anew. Their very name, even, cannot be accepted in France, at least where their very termination is suggestive of alkaloids or glucosides, and it will not do again to commit the mistake which Bonjean has perpetuated, to the confusion of therapeutic nomenclature, by giving to the hydro-alcoholic extract of ergot the name of ergotin. I propose, however, on this occasion to employ the terms in ordinary use, as, in fact, is done in the case of podophyllin, and to say baptisin, euonymin, etc. This terminology, moreover, is adhered to despite the fact that chemists have already described under the names of juglandin, euonymin, iridin, hydrastin, certain substances which are veritable alkaloids. One of my pupils, Dr. Daret, has made a careful study of these new cholagogues, the first, in fact, that has been undertaken in France.*

I here place before you samples of several comparatively new pharmaceutical products which I have obtained in England, and of which I am enabled to

---

* G. Daret on Certain New Cholagogues of Vegetable Origin (Thése de Paris, 1880).

give you a summary description, owing to the kindness of my excellent interne in pharmacy, M. Jaillet, who has examined them.

Here is a sample of euonymin. It is, as you see, a greenish powder, of strong, rank odor, insoluble in water, slightly soluble in alcohol and ether, and which is obtained from a species of wahoo, the euonymus atro-purpureus, much prized in our gardens by reason of the beautiful color of its leaves. It is an oleo-resin, which burns readily, and which must not be confounded with the *euonymin*, a species of mannite, studied by Kubel, Roederer, and Grunner. The latter is a crystalline substance, obtained from the enonymus Europæus.

In France euonymin is often found under the form of a brown powder; the difference in color is owing to the part of the plant from which the resin has been extracted. In England the leaves and stalk are utilized; in France the root.

This substance, which, according to experimenters is one of our best cholagogues, and which has received honorable mention in the U. S. Dispensatory, is given in the dose of ten to twenty centigrammes (two to four grains). You do not obtain from it a very decided purgative action, but its cholagogue effect is quite marked. I have myself prescribed it with success in cases of catarrhal icterus, and in dysentery. Moreover, in France Henri Gueneau de Mussy, who was the first to introduce these medicaments, has derived good effects from it, and Dr. Blondeau has reported a case of pseudo-membranous enteritis in which euonymin produced excellent results.

The euonymus is chiefly known in the U. S. under the name of wahoo, a name given it by the Indians.

The plant has also been named *spindle tree* and *burning bush*. It is a tall, erect shrub, with small dark-purple flowers, in cymes, in axillary peduncles. The wahoo is indigenous in the northern and western states. Euonymin in this country is obtained from the dried bark by reducing it to powder, agitating with chloroform a tincture made with dilute alcohol, separating the chloroformic solution, and allowing it to evaporate, and by a further process of purification; the euonymin thus obtained is uncrystallizable, and intensely bitter. Dr. Geo. B. Wood speaks of it as tonic, hydragogue, cathartic, antiperiodic and cholagogue, although he regards its action as somewhat uncertain.

A fluid extract is much used; dose, a dessert to a tablespoonful. The euonymus is a favorite with the eclectics.—[Trans.]

This blackish powder with shiny particles is iridin, an oleo-resin extracted from iris versicolor. Wood and Bache mention it, and Rutherford ranks it along with euonymin among the very best cholagogues. It has given me the same results as euonymin, and from a therapeutic view I regard it as of about equal merit.

Iris versicolor (blue flag) is found in all parts of the U. S. in low wet places and on the borders of swamps, which it adorns by its large and beautiful flowers. The root is the medicinal part. Blue flag possesses cathartic, emetic, diuretic and cholagogue properties. It is, however, little used by the profession at large.

The dose of the dried root is from ten to twelve grains. "Under the unscientific name of *iridin* or *irisin*, which should be reserved for the active principle when discovered, the eclectics have obtained an oleoresin, got by precipitating the tincture of the root with water and mixing the result with some absorbent powder, such as licorice root. This may be given in the form of a pill in the dose of three or four grains. It is thought to unite cholagogue and diuretic with aperient properties."—[Wood and Bache.]

This yellowish powder, which I now show you, with strong and rank odor resembling podophylilin, is *baptisin*, which is extracted from the wild indigo, Baptisia tinctoria; it is a medicament similar to the preceding, and the dose, according to Wood and Bache, is 2 grains at bed time.

The Baptisia tinctoria is an indigenous plant found all over the United States, abounding in woods and uplands. The whole plant becomes black when dried, and has been used for dyeing purposes, known by the name of "dyers' weed." The root, which is the medicinal part most in use, has a nauseous, bitter and somewhat acrid taste. Baptisin, which is an impure extract, is emetic and cathartic in large doses, laxative in small doses.

Rutherford has experimented with it in dogs in the dose of six or seven grains; it produces considerable congestion of the stomach and intestines.

I here show you a specimen of hydrastin, the alcoholic extract of Hydrastis Canadensis, which you must not confound with the *crystallized hydrastin*, which is a real alkaloid, discovered by Durand, and studied by Perrins and Mahla. It is a decided cholagogue, and more of a purgative than the preceding preparation. This, by the way, is one of the most curious facts connected with the experiment of Rutherford, *i. e.*, the discovery of these non-purgative cholagogues which augment the biliary secretion without increasing the number of stools, and in the employment of which it is necessary to add a true purgative, such as sulphate of soda, for instance.

Hydrastin is a resinous alcoholic extract of the root of hydrastis Canadensis. It presents itself under the form of a brown powder, of bitter and astringent taste. It is soluble in alcohol and in ether, little soluble in water, soluble in chloroform. This gum-resin readily burns, and gives all the characters of a resin. It is probable that the alkaloid discovered in 1861 in the same plant by Durand is contained in this gum-resin. Durand's hydrastin (hydrastia W. and B.) which has been studied by Perrin and Mahla, crystallizes in white spiny prisms and melts at 135° C. (275° F.) Heated on platinum foil, it burns with a sooty flame. It is insoluble in water, soluble in alcohol, ether, and dilute mineral acids. Hydrastin is associated with berberine in the roots of the hydrastis Canadensis.

This specimen of juglandin which I here place before you under the form of a black powder has a special oily odor resembling that of decayed nuts; as its name indicates, it is an extract of the Juglans cinerea and belongs to the group above mentioned, being a cholagogue medicament without being a purgative. À propos of this substance, I must remind you that Tanret has found in the butternut an alkaloid which he has called *juglandin*, and that Luton has recommended in the treatment of tuberculous meningitis an alcoholic extract of the juglans under the name of extract of Granval.*

[Podophyllum peltatum (described in "Diseases of the Stomach and Intestines) is a perennial plant of the Berberidaceæ family, growing in North America. The parts employed are the rhizomes and roots, from which a resin is extracted called podophyllin, which presents itself under the aspect of a brilliant powder of yellowish brown color, and acrid, bitter taste.

According to Mayer, besides this resin, podophyllin contains berberine, a colorless alkaloid, a special acid, an odorous matter and saponine. The resin is soluble in alcohol, ether, the essential oils, bisulphide of carbon, and in part in the alkalies. In the dose of from ⅓ to 1 grain, podophyllin provokes regular stools ten to twelve hours after its administration. Large doses (1 to 2 grains) are likely to produce nausea and vomiting as well as colic.]

This powder with shiny particles which I here place before you is leptandrin, an impure resinoid extract of the Leptandria veronica. Reeb, of Phalsbourg has recommended it along with podophyllin in

---

*Tanret's juglandin is in the form of long needles; this substance exists in the leaves of the butternut combined with tannin. The juglandin of commerce is an alcoholic extract of the butternut, and comes in the form of little lumps of a brownish color; dose, 2 to 5 grains.

the treatment of dysentery, and Lloyd has made a special study of this resin.*

Here is a sample of sanguinarin, an impure extract from the Sanguinaria Canadensis. We are already acquainted with an alkaloid derived from this same plant, *Sanguinarine*. The product now before you is a cholagogue with but slight purgative properties. According to Rutherford, it excites the secretion of the liver, giving rise to a flow of watery bile; the dose is from one-half grain to a grain.

Lastly, this powder, of a dirty grey, earthy color and saltish taste, is phytolaccin, a resin which is obtained from a plant which grows in abundance in North America, the Phytolacca decandra. It will not do to confound this product with the *phytolaccine* studied by Claassen, which is a glucoside; the pre-

---

* Lloyd, American Journal of Pharmacy, 1880.

Leptandrin is of rank nauseous odor, bitter somewhat sweetish but nauseous taste. According to Lloyd, Mayne and Mayer, the resin precipitated from the alcoholic extract of the Leptandria, does not contain the active principle of this plant to this must be added the precipitate thrown down by sulphuric acid from the liquid which has furnished the resin; this precipitate contains an impure glucocide.

Reeb, a pharmacist of Phalsbourg, made a study of leptandrin in 1875. According to him, this substance has feeble laxative properties, in large doses producing frequent evacuations. He has employed it in conjunction with podophyllin in epidemic dysentery; it may also be given, he says, in this disease associated with camphor and quinine.

paration before you, in large doses, is both purgative and emetic, while in smaller doses (one to three grains) it is both cholagogue and purgative.

What is the true value of these substances with which Rutherford, according to the expression of Gueneau de Mussy, has enriched the armamentarium of the physician? What is to be their future? The first trials which I have made in Cochin hospital with these substances, obtained directly from Edinburgh, have shown that, with the exception of euonymin, hydrastin, and perhaps iridin and phytolaccin, there is little to expect from these novelties, and that they are largely impure, ill-defined substances, demanding both from a chemical and pharmaceutical point of view, a more complete investigation.

To these complex products, these oleo resins, I would join two well-defined medicinal agents which seem to possess great activity as cholagogues: Colchicine, which, according to Garrod, has a marked action on the liver, and aconitine, which, also as Laborde and Gellé have shown, also acts powerfully on the biliary secretion.

Colchicine is an extract of the colchicum autumnale, it is crystalline, inodorous, with sharp bitter taste, soluble in water, alcohol and ether.

There is also an amorphous colchicine, which is neutral and uncrystallizable, not forming definite salts, and breaking up, under the influence of acids, into colchiceine and a resinous substance. Tannate of colchicine has been extolled as remedial in gout.

Garrod employs only the amorphous colchicine. The dose would be two to four milligrammes in water or in some aromatic infusion.

As for the cholagogues of mineral origin, I shall rapidly pass in review the new facts brought to light by the experiments of Rutherford. These experiments have taught us that salicylate of sodium is a powerful excitant of the biliary secretion, and it occupies the third rank in the scale of cholagogues.

According to Rutherford, the action of sodium salicylate on the intestine is very feeble, hence, when given with cholagogue intent, the dose should be administered at bedtime, and followed the next morning by a dose of Glauber's salts.

The phosphate and especially the sulphate of sodium are also excellent cholagogues, and thus is explained the favorable action of certain sodic sulphate mineral waters, and especially of Carlsbad, on hepatic affections. The double tartrate of potassium and sodium, Rochelle salts (sal de Seignette), is also a good cholagogue.

But while the salts of sodium augment the biliary secretion, those of magnesium on the contrary, and especially the sulphate of magnesia, diminish this secretion, according to the experiments of Rutherford. We ought then, if we accept this experimental datum, to substitute as a purgative in affections of the liver sulphate of sodium for sulphate of magnesium.

We have already seen the contradictions which exist between clinical and physiological experimentation in reference to the action of calomel; there is the same want of agreement relative to the action of the alkaline carbonates on the biliary secretion.

Clinical experimentation in almost numberless instances says that the alkaline carbonates, and in particular the sodic carbonate waters, such as Vichy, have a curative action in affections of the liver, and physiological experimentation replies that instead of increasing the secretion of bile, they diminish it. We admit the claims of the experimental physiologist without discarding the results of the clinic. Doubtless the secretion of bile is not augmented, but the alkalies, in modifying the functions of nutrition, in regulating the digestive functions, in calming all inflammatory states of the disordered mucosa, in acting on the circulation of the liver and modifying the bile, have certainly a manifest action on the excretion of the bile, and on the hepatic gland.

Moreover, if experimentation shows us that the alkalies have no action on the liver as the organ of the biliary secretion, recent experimental researches conducted by Martin Damourette and Hyades* have put in clear light the undoubted action of alkalies on the augmentation of the figure of urea secreted in the twenty-four hours, and for this reason their beneficial effect on the liver considered as the principal organ of urea formation.†

---

*Acad. des Sciences, March, 1880. "On the Nutritive Effects of Alkalies in Large Doses."

† Martin Damourette and Hyades have shown the

As you see, from the point of view of the treatment of diseases of the liver, it is not sufficient that experimentation shall have pronounced more or less definitely on a medicament, to warrant the medical profession in at once adopting these conclusions as a datum of practice; it is necessary that clinical experience shall confirm the results of experimentation, and I cannot point you to a more striking proof of this than the facts which I have just stated relative to cholagogues.

How are we to explain the cholagogue action of the substances which we have just examined? We may suppose it to be due to the irritation determined by these substances on the duodenum, and thus compare what takes place in the liver with what takes place in the salivary glands when you irritate the buccal cavity. At the same time this explanation does not seem sufficient, and for this reason: we have seen

---

undoubted effects of alkalies, and in particular of the natural alkaline waters, on nutrition. According to them, these alkalies are trophic agents in quantities equal to a bottle of Vichy water per day. They energize nutrition in helping the entire series of acts which constitute it, and they notably increase the figure of the blood globules and favor disassimilation, as is proved by the augmentation of urea and diminution of uric acid in the urine. Alkalies are then promoters of disassimilation (nutritifs déperditeurs) after the manner of muscular exercise, hydrotherapy and inhalations of oxygen.

that there are substances which are cholagogue without being purgative, and vice versa.

Rutherford, on the other hand, has shown that the more a substance is purgative the less it is cholagogue; thus it is that purgatives which are the highest in the scale, drastics for instance, are medicines which diminish rather than increase the biliary secretion.

Can we affirm that it is by acting on the circulation of the liver that the special effect of these medicaments is produced, and that every medicament which has for its property to congest this organ should be ranked in the group of cholagogues? This explanation hardly meets the requirement, for we have seen that certain cholagogues really lessen the circulation in the liver. We are, in fact, reduced to the supposition that it is by acting directly on the hepatic cells, or on the secretory nerves which preside over the function of the organ, that the substances act which we have just passed in review.

In order that you may better remember what I have just said, I here place before you a couple of tables which I have borrowed from Gueneau de Mussy, tables in which are grouped the different medicaments according to their cholagogue power. The figure which accompanies each substance is its biliary coefficient, *i. e.*, the quantity of bile obtained per hour and per kilogramme of the animal weight.

ACTIVITY OF THE BILIARY SECRETION BEFORE AND AFTER THE
INTRODUCTION INTO· THE DUODENUM OF THE SUB-
STANCES UNDER EXPERIMENTATION.

	Before.	After.	Difference.
Aloes (average of the differences, 0.61)	0.26	0 93	67
	0.34	0.69	35
Podophyllin, average, 0.46	0.52	1.01	49
	0.04	0.47	43
Salicylate of sodium, average, 0.455	0.32	0.89	57
	0.26	0.66	40
Extract of physostigma, average, 0.455	0.13	0.75	62 .
	0.09	0.36	27
Benzoate of Sodium, Single experiment, 0.42	0.22	0.64	42
Sanguinaria, average, 0.404	0.07	0.48	39
	0.16	0.40	24
	0.12	0.30	18
Iridin, average, 0.36	0.16	0.63	47
	0.23	0 53	31
Bichloride of mercury, average, 0.32	0.22	0.85	63
	0.20	0.55	35
	0.17	0.47	32
	0.48	0.72	24
Euonymin, average, 0.30	0.07	0.46	39
	0.25	0.47	22
Benzoate of ammonia, single experiment, 0.30	0.24	0.54	30
Nitro-muriatic acid, single experiment	0.11	0.39	28
Ipecac, average, 0.255	0.24	0.55	31
	0.18	0.38	20
Juglandin, single experiment, 0.22	0.10	0.32	22
Colchicum, average, 0.21	0.13	0.45	32
	0.10	0.20	10
Hydrastin, average, 0.186	0.10	0.32	38
	0.10	0.28	18
	0.23	0.38	15

ACTIVITY OF THE BILIARY SECRETION BEFORE AND AFTER THE
INTRODUCTION INTO THE DUODENUM OF THE SUB-
STANCES UNDER EXPERIMENTATION.

	Before	After.	Difference.
Phosphate of sodium, single experiment, 0.17......................	0.20	0.44	17
Baptisin, average, 0.165...........	0.12	0.28	17
	0.23	0'39	6
Leptandrin, average, 0.155...... ..	0.19	0.27	8
	0.08	0.21	23
Jalap, average, 0.155..............	0.17	0.35	18
	0.16	0,29	13
Rhubarb, single experiment, 0.15...	0.17	0.32	15
Sulphate of potassium, single experiment. 0.15......................	0.32	0 47	15
Colocynth, average, 0.135.	0.29	0.45	16
	0.16	0.27	11
Sulphate of sodium, average, 0.14..	0.25	0.38	13
	0.10	0.25	15
Rochelle salt, single experiment, 0.10...........................			

I have largely drawn from Rutherford's important physiological work, but I repeat, with certain reservations which I desire again to emphasize in fin-
ishing this lecture. These reservations pertain to
the therapeutic value of these different substances.
You have seen that with respect to the sodic-bicarbon-
ate waters, as well as to calomel we have had to give
the precedence to the clinic, over experimentation;
this precedence ought always to be insisted upon, and
before adopting certain cholagogues, as yet unknown
to medical practice, it will be best to wait till, by
numerous clinical observations, such new medicaments

have merited the dignity of a place in the materia
medica, and in the physician's drug case.

These data having been settled, we will now enter
on the study of the therapeutics of diseases of the
liver, and begin with the treatment of biliary lithiasis,
which will be the subject of the next lecture.*

---

*ACTIVITYGIVEN TO THE SECRETION OF BILE BY DIFFERENT SUB-
STANCES ACCORDING TO THE EXPERIMENTS OF RUTHERFORD.

Figures expressing the excess of secretion excited by
these substances:

Aloes	0.67	Benzoate of ammonia	0.30
Bichloride of mercury	0.63	Nitro-muriatic acid	0.28
Physostigma	0.62	Physostigma	0.27
Salicylate of soda	0.57	Sanguinaria	0.26
Iridin	0.47	Hydrastin	0.23
Podophyllin	0.43	Leptandrin	0.23
Benzoate of soda	0.42	Juglandin	0.22
Salicylate of soda	0.40	Euonymin	0.22
Euonymin	0.39	Ipecac	0.20
Sanguinarin	0.39	Jalap	0.18
Aloes	0.39	Hydrastin	0.18
Corrosive sublimate	0.35	Sanguinaria	0.18
Colchicum	0.32	Phosphate of sodium	0.17
Ipecac	0.31	Baptisin	0.17
Colocynth	0.15	Baptisin	0.16
Sulphate of potassium	0.15	Sulphate of sodium	0.13
Hydrastin	0.15	Jalap	0.13
Rhubarb	0.15	Colocynth	0.11
Phytolaccine	0.15	Colchicum	0.10
Phytolaccine	0.14	Leptandrin	0.08
Corrosive Sublimate	0.30	Rochelle salt	0.10

CHAPTER III.

TREATMENT OF BILIARY LITHIASIS.

SUMMARY.—Anatomy and the Physiology of the Bile Ducts—Hepatic, Cystic, Choledic Ducts—The Gall Bladder—Structure of the Bile Ducts—The Muscular Layer—Biliary Calculi, Their Composition—Chemical Causes of the Production of Calculi—Individual Causes—Influence of Sex, of Regimen, of Exercise, of Diatheses — Pathological Physiology of Hepatic Colic—Spasm of the Bile Ducts—Indications and Treatment of Biliary Lithiasis—Treatment of Hepatic Colic—Subcutaneous Injections of Morphine—Chloral and Chloroform—Adjuvant Means—Lithontriptics—Durande's Remedy—Action of Alkaline Mineral Waters—Cholagogue Medication—Hygienic Treatment of Biliary Lithiasis.

GENTLEMEN:—Biliary lithiasis is a frequent affection which gives rise, as you know, to certain acute symptoms known under the name of hepatic colic, for which a prompt and energetic treatment is demanded; therefore I shall make this subject a part of my present course, and dwell at some length upon it. But, in order that you may well understand the value and utility of the therapeutic agents recommended in such cases, I must enter somewhat into anatomical and physiological details concerning the bile ducts and the biliary calculi which pass through them.

I shall be brief in my description of the bile ducts. You remember the course of the hepatic duct, which takes its origin in the liver by that network of biliary canaliculi, which, as we have seen in one of the preceding lectures, surrounds the hepatic cells. After a short transit, this duct meets the cystic duct from the gall bladder, and both unite into one duct, the ductus choledochus, and empty into the duodenum by the ampulla of Vater. I shall say little concerning the bile duct, with whose anatomy you are sufficiently familiar; but there is one point to which I desire especially to call your attention, *viz:* the intimate structure of these bile ducts.

As for the mucous membrane, there is general agreement among anatomists; it presents little valves or folds, especially in the neighborhood of the cystic duct, which are called valves of Heister; moreover, this mucosa has glands in greater or less abundauce. There is not the same agreement respecting the fibromuscular structure of these ducts, and in some experiments undertaken about fifteen years ago, I was led to make an attentive study of this question.*

I had been impressed by the disagreements of histologists on this point. In fact, while certain anatomists, as Sappey, assign to these excretory bile ducts a muscular coating rich in unstriped fibres, and Fort even describes as pertaining to this coat three layers with variable directions, others, on the contrary,

---

* Dujardin-Beaumetz, "A Study of Spasm of the Bile Ducts."—(Bull de Therap., 1873.)

as Kolliker, Leydig, Frey, and Virchow, affirm that there is not any muscular layer properly so-called in these ducts; they scarcely even admit that any exist even in the gall bladder.

In order to decide this contention, I prevailed upon two histologists whom I have the honor to have had for pupils, Prof. Renaut, of Lyons, and Prof. Grancher, to study anew this question. The results of their labors were decisive; both show that there undoubtedly exist smooth muscular fibres in the bile ducts, and that these muscular fibres are disseminated throughout the fasciculi of connective and elastic tissue constituting the fibrous coat of these ducts; moreover, they put in clear light this fact, already long known, that inflammation taking place in the duct augments this muscular layer; Bouisson, Herard, Deville, and Broca, have, in fact, shown that in pathological cases this stratum may become hypertrophied.*

---

* Below the epithelium you find a very thin layer with a small number of oval nuclei scattered throughout its substance, a layer, essentially of connective tissue fibres, and very adherent to the subjacent tissue; this tissue, which forms the limiting membrane of the ductus choledochus, is remarkable for its richness in fine elastic fibres thickly set in a connective tissue very poor in cells. In proportion as your dissection embraces the deeper tissues of the choledochus, the elastic connective tissue changes, and the reciprocal disposition of these elements is modified; we find bundles of true connective tissue and interlaced undulating elastic fibres resembling the same elements existing in the subcutaneous connective tissue.

It is probable that it is with one of these pathological cases that Martin had to do in his examination
of the choledic duct, when he claims to have found
two planes of muscular fibres, the one internal,
longitudinal, the other external, of circular fibres. So
then, it is well settled that the excretory bile ducts are
fibro-muscular tubes which are the seat of more or less
energetic contractions, as has been shown by the researches of Audigé, of Laborde and myself. You
will see later the capital importance of these facts.

Laborde has shown that under the influence of induc-
tion currents the gall-bladder and even the bile ducts,
hepatic, cystic, and choledic, undergo a slow but very manifest contraction.

Let us now examine the calculi which sometimes
pass through these ducts. They offer a variable
volume, and their number is variable also. In the
vast majority of cases they are constituted by cholesterine or bile pigment, forming stratified layers of dif-

---

It is by an insensible transition that this difference of
appearance between the elastic fibres and simple connective
tissue fibres presents itself as you dissect away from the
cavity of the duct.

We may then divide the wall proper of the choledochus
into three coats which are insensibly blended: an internal connective and sub-epithelial coat, a middle coat of very close
elastic fibres, and an external coat of connective tissue
bundles and undulating elastic fibres. It is in this last coat
that we find here and there a few scattered elements of smooth
muscular fibres.

5 *

ferent colors, according as they are more or less tinted by bilirubin.

The number of calculi is very variable. Ordinarily from five to twenty are found in the gall bladder. In other cases they are single; in other cases a considerable number are met with. In a woman, 61 years of age, Frerichs counted 1950. Morgagni has counted 3000, Hoffman 3606, and in the collection of Osto there is a gall bladder containing 7802 calculi.

All the calculi contained in the gall bladder, whatever the number, are of the same chemical composition, color and structure. Their size is variable, from a grain of millet seed to a hen's egg. Fauconneau-Dufresne has divided gall stones into three classes:

1. Those of small size from a grain of sand to a small pea.

2. Middle size, from a small pea up to a filbert.

3. Large size, from a filbert up to a hen's egg.

The calculi may be olivary, pisiform, lenticular, polyhedric, cylindric, cubic, finger shaped, have the form of dice, of coins, of pyramids, etc. They may be smooth, hollow and striated, etc. But the ordinary typical form is the olive-shaped. The solitary calculi are roundish or ovoid. Multiple calculi ordinarily present facets, which appear to be due to the massing together of the calculi, and not to the friction of one upon another, for you do not often find, on examining gall stones, any interruption in the lamellæ which constitute them, which would be apt to take place if the facet was the result of friction.

Nevertheless, in 1851, Barth found in the gall bladder of a woman of 63 years, a dozen irregular calculi, with rough surfaces; he remarked that certain of these calculi had been broken and a little worn by friction. Other observers have recorded similar facts. Some have found in the gall bladder, not stones properly so called, but a thick pasty whitish mass composed almost entirely of cholesterine (Besnier), or even a biliary sediment of the consistence of mud (Durand-Fardel).

Ordinarily, however, the biliary concretions are quite consistent, although they are marked easily by the finger nail; the hardest calculi are those of cholesterine.

The structure of the calculi is variable, and has been well studied by numerous authorities, who have differently divided these biliary concretions. Walter's classification is: 1st. The striated calculi, transparent or opaque, which may be either smooth or anfractuous; 2nd. The lamellated calculi, whose substance is disposed in layers around a nucleus; 3rd. Calculi enveloped by a cortex.—Hein's classification is "simple calculi;" 2, "composite calculi."

Frerichs divides calculi into: 1. Simple homogenous calculi, whose structure is uniform, whose fracture presents an earthy, soapy, or crystalline surface, and which have neither nucleus nor cortex. 2. Composite calculi presenting a central nucleus surrounded by a zone more or less thick, and covered by a cortex. The nucleus, brown or black, is composed of colepyrrhine and lime, cholate of lime, or of cholesterine.

The nucleus, ordinarily single and central, is sometimes excentric. There may even be in a calculus several nuclei. In a dry state these nuclei may undergo a sort of retraction, become split or even fragmented. The smaller the calculus, as a rule, the larger the nucleus.

Cases have been mentioned in which the nucleus was constituted by a foreign body, such as a lumbricus or blood clot. The middle layer, immediately surrounding the nucleus, is generally striated, and constituted by crystals of cholesterine, pure or mingled with pigment.

Concentric zones are also generally observed, indicating the growth of the calculus by successive strata.

The cortex is generally more or less thick, sometimes

smooth and sometimes mammillated, but it is clearly distinguished from the middle layer by its color, its stratified appearance and its consistence. It is formed either of cholesterine, of bile pigment or of lime.

Biliary calculi are formed at the expense of the elements of the bile; rarely they are composed of a single substance, they are ordinarily mixed. Cholesterine is generally the basis of these stones; next in the order of frequency come bile pigment and lime salts.

Charles Robin divides calculi into calculi of cholesterine and calculi of coloring matter. Those of cholesterine pure are colorless or pearly white. Subjected on platinum foil to a lamp flame, they first melt, then burn like a fatty substance, giving off a sooty light. If the calculus is composed of pure cholesterine, there remains no residue on the platinum foil. Insoluble in caustic potash and soda, they are very soluble in boiling alcohol and in ether. A drop of this ethereal solution under the microscope gives colorless rhomboidal plates by evaporation.

Concentrated H_2SO_4 colors these calculi yellow, and boiling nitric acid transforms them into cholesteric acid.

The calculi of the coloring matter of the bile (biliverdine and cholepyrrhine) are brown, black or dark, deep green or greenish, according to the quantity of coloring matter. They do not melt when heated, they burn without flame, and leave a sooty residue. They are insoluble in ether and alkaline liquids. Treated by nitric acid, they pass successively through different shades of colors; green, blue, violet, red and yellow. To ascertain the composition of the calculi, Luton, of Rheims, has proposed a very simple method of analysis, which consists in subjecting a portion of the calculus to the action of solvents, hot alcohol, for instance, then allowing it to become cold; crystallization takes place and the microscope enables you to recognize the principal constituent elements of the calculus;

rhomboidal plates of cholesterine, needles and bacillary crystals of cholate of lime, etc., etc. The following is a recent . analysis of a biliary calculus of a woman thirty-four years of age (Bettmann):

Cholesterine.........	79.00
Fatty matters.....	0.80
Water	7.41
Mineral elements....	3.23
Glycocholate and taurocholate of soda..............	5.28
Mucus and coloring matters	2.69
Loss...........	0.73

Under the name of biliary gravel, Fauconneau-Dufresne classes only such concretions as are under the size of the smallest lentil, and which present no appearance of structure. He gives three varieties: cholesteric gravel, pigmentary gravel, and melanic or carbonaceous gravel.

I have said that the size is variable; in fact from the calculus which is as large as a hen's egg and fills the gall bladder, down to the little grains of sand constituting what Fauconneau-Dufresne calls hepatic gravel, you will find gall stones of all dimensions.

You may also find calcareous concretions in the ducts; but this is a matter which it is not a part of our present plan to treat of, for this calcareous lithiasis never takes place except when, from some cause, the gall bladder becomes obliterated. These calculi, then, play no part in the production of hepatic colic, which is our present subject. What it is of importance for us to know is the pathology of these calculi, for if we understand the first cause of their production, we shall be able, from a therapeutic standpoint, to oppose their formation.

I have said that the calculi are constituted by deposits of cholesterine; what are the circumstances which lead to the precipitation of cholesterine ? We have to study the two following causes: either the cholesterine is precipitated because it is in excess in the bile, or the proportion of cholesterine remains normal, but the other elements of the bile undergo modification and lead to precipitation of the latter.

Let us take up the cases where cholesterine is in excess, and here you must recall to mind what you know concerning its origin. Physiologists, as I have told you, are agreed in accepting Flint's conclusions, deduced from his careful experiments, and in considering this substance as a product of disassimilation of the nervous system. This experimental datum seems to be confirmed, in a certain measure, by clinical experience, for it is principally in women with highly developed nervous systems that you observe biliary lithiasis; and for my part, the more my attention has been directed to this explanation, the more firm is my conviction as to its truth.

It is chiefly young women, nervous and impressible, who are the subjects of hepatic colic. It is probable that in these cases the too active exercise of the cerebro-spinal axis explains the excessive production of cholesterine and its precipitation in consequence of over-production, and I am convinced that this circumstance has not been sufficiently taken account of by the different authorities who have considered this question.

The second cause of the precipitation of cholesterine, *i. e.*, the modifications of its vehicle, the quantity of this substance remaining the same, has been
studied by Thénard, who has indicated, as a factor
which may bring about this precipitation, the diminution of the salts of sodium. Moreover, Bramson has
shown that the appearance of lime in the bile may
cause the precipitation of the coloring matter. Lastly,
the bile which in the normal state is alkaline may become acid, and this is especially likely to take place
under the influence of animal diet; and acid bile
favors the precipitation of cholesterine.

Moreover, as we frequently find a nucleus of
mucus in these calculi, we must assign an important
rôle to the inflammations of the bile ducts; these inflammations cause a hyper-secretion of mucus which
may give rise to a nucleus, around which the cholesterine deposits itself.

Such are the physical and chemical causes which
favor the production of calculi. Let us now inquire
what are the individual causes.

Women, as you know, are the most frequent subjects of biliary lithiasis, for statistics show that twice
as many women as men suffer from this disease.
(Durand-Fardel's statistics (1868) show that out of 230
cases, 142 were women, and 88 were men. Senac's
statistics, out of a total of 311 individuals, give 227
women). With reference to individual causes, an important part has been assigned to diet; it has been

maintained that a too fatty regimen is one of the most prolific causes of biliary calculi. I believe this statement to be somewhat overdrawn. It has not, in fact, been proved, either by experimental or chemical observations, that a diet exclusively of fatty food predisposes more than any other to biliary lithiasis, and the observations which have been made among people living on oleaginous food, as the people of the far north, the Norwegians, the Esquimaux, etc., do not prove that they are more subject to hepatic colic than other nations which consume less of fatty substances.

But if the influence of these fatty aliments is not demonstrated, there is another factor which in my opinion plays an important part in pathogeny, namely, allowing too long an interval to elapse between meals. Physiology in fact teaches that during digestion the bile flows in great abundance into the duodenum, and that the gall bladder nearly or quite empties itself at this time. We know also that one of the predominant causes of the precipitation of cholesterine in the bile is the prolonged sojourn of that liquid in the gall bladder. When the meals are too far apart, or when, as is the practice of some persons, only one meal a day is eaten, the gall bladder is placed in a favorable condition for the precipitation of cholesterine.

There is another factor which also aids the flow of bile, viz., the respiratory movements, which by the pressure which they effect upon the gall bladder and the intestinal mass through the intermediation of the diaphragm tend to empty the gall bladder. Hence the influence of want of exercise on the production of these calculi is apparent, and it is in fact, sedentary persons whom we find to be the most subject to biliary lithiasis. Add that active respiratory movements favor the combustion of fatty matters, and you easily understand why we assign the first place to exercise in the hygiene of lithiasis.*

The diatheses have a notable influence on the production of biliary lithiasis, and despite the opposition of Durand-Fardel to the doctrine of Willemin who maintains that biliary lithiasis, like urinary lithiasis, depends on the uric diathesis, it is none the less true that we find more cases of biliary calculi among the arthritic than among any other class of people.

Heredity seems also to play a prominent part in biliary lithiasis. Petit and Willemin cite examples, as also do Budd and Fauconneau-Dufresne.

Senac, in studying the family health and constitution of patients who have consulted him, has so often met with different manifestations of the arthritic diathesis, that he believes this diathesis to be an important factor in biliary lithiasis.

To the support of this view, he brings forward a certain

---

* Consult the following authorities: Budd on Diseases of the Liver, London, 1857; Frerich's, on Diseases of the Liver, Wm. Wood & Co., 1879; Fauconneau-Dufresne, Treatise on Calculous Affections of the Liver; Willemin, on the Treatment of Hepatic Colic by Vichy Water, Beneke in Deutsch. Archiv. f. Klin. Med., 1876, etc., etc.

number of observations which seem to place the matter beyond all doubt.

According to Senac, individuals smitten with hepatic colic are not attacked in a state of health; the hepatic disease either succeeds existing pathological states or adds itself to states that have previously existed. Migraine, uric lithiasis, diathetic coryzas, hemorrhoids with or without hemorrhage, acute or chronic arthrites of rheumatic or gouty nature, urticaria, eczema, acne rosacea, etc.; pregnancy, accouchement, menstruation, the menopause, suppression of a bloody flux or an habitual discharge, forced rest, the depressing moral emotions, affections of the liver, in fact all causes capable of modifying the hepatic circulation, may, it is said, determine the outbreak of hepatic colic.

Beneke has also set forth the relation which exists between atheromatous degeneration of the arteries and biliary lithiasis. He has found that in three-fourths of his cases (350 autopsies made by him at Marbourg) there was atheromatous degeneration of the arteries along with biliary lithiasis.* To sum up, all the facts go to prove, as Bouchard has well shown, that the cause of biliary calculi resides essentially and primarily in a general disturbance of nutrition†.

---

* Beneke, Gallensteintildung Atheromatose Arterienentartung und Fettsbildung (Arch. f. Klin. Med., 1876).

† This is the way Bouchard expresses himself: "Biliary lithiasis manifests itself only in individuals whose nutrition is retarded; in those affected with that nutritive vice of which one of the consequences is to prevent the destruction of acids, and to cause their accumulation in the organism, to diminish the alkalinity of the humors, to take lime from the anatomical elements, and with it impregnate the liquids of excretion." (Maladies par Ralentissement de la Nutrition, p. 85).

We know now the causes which are operative in the formation of calculi, and we have studied the anatomy of the bile ducts. Let us now consider the mode of passage of gall stones in the different ducts, and the accidents which may result from their presence. In the immense majority of cases, calculi form in the gall bladder; this is where the major part of the bile accumulates and sojourns; nevertheless, in certain circumstances true biliary gravel has been known to be deposited in the hepatic bile ducts and to manifest its presence in the radicles of the hepatic duct and in the hepatic duct itself. But such facts are exceptional; ordinarily the calculus, when formed in the gall bladder, may increase in size and remain there a long time without determining any symptom, and this is so true that at the autopsies of the aged women at the Salpêtrière, it may be said that it is the rule to find in the gall bladder calculi more or less voluminous, without any disturbance having been noted during life therefrom. But at other times, calculi of little size pass with the bile into the cystic duct and thence into the ductus choledochus, and are voided by the intestine.

These calculi may make their journey from the gall bladder to the intestine without causing any attack of colic, and in my own practice I observed several years ago, a very curious instance in one of my patients who had been passing by stool a considerable quantity of biliary gravel without ever feeling any colicky pains. At the same time, there generally ensues an aggregate of painful symptoms described under the name of hepatic colic.

In 1873, I made with Dr. Audigé (a) numerous experiments in order to obtain a clearer understanding of the way these gall stones pass through the biliary passages. We first of all discovered in animals that the bile ducts when irritated are the seat of a real spasm, which is, moreover, easily explained, if you recall to mind the anatomical structure of these ducts. Then we artificially reproduced the attack of hepatic colic, for after having introduced into the common bile duct of dogs by the intestinal opening certain foreign bodies, we observed the extreme sensibility of these conduits in these animals and the mode of passage of the calculi, which by reason of the spasmodic movement of which the ducts are the seat, either travel towards the intestine or gall bladder.*

This is a fact of capital importance, which even justifies the affirmation that when, in persons affected with biliary colic, you do not find the offending body

---

(a) Dujardin-Reaumetz, Étude sur le spasme des voies biliaires, à propos du traitement de la eolique hépatique (Bull. de thérap., 1873, t. LXXXV, p. 305).—Audigé, Researches expérimentales sur le spasme des voies biliaires, à propos du traitement de la colique hépatique. Thése de Paris, 1874.

* These are the conclusions of the thesis of Audige:

(1). The treatment of hepatic colic should consist in diminishing the contraction of the bile ducts and the pain therefrom resulting: (2). Anæsthetics and morphine employed subcutaneously fulfill this end."

—the *corps du délit*—in the stools, you should not at once conclude that the calculus does not exist, and make the diagnosis of hepatalgia. It may happen, in fact, that the calculus, after having traversed the ductus choledochus a part of the way towards its intestinal opening, shall return to its starting point and fall back into the gall bladder.

These experimental researches, which have since been confirmed by Laborde, demonstrate that in hepatic colic there is a veritable painful spasm of the bile ducts.*

---

* These are the conclusions of the work of M. Laborde:

1. The bile ducts are endowed with contractility, and may consequently enter into a state of spasm under the influence of an excitation direct or indirect; this contractility is of the same kind as that pertaining to the smooth muscular fibres of organic life, and the existence of these fibres in the bile ducts is demonstrated both by histological examination and experimental physiology.

2. The mucous membrane of these ducts is endowed with a very high sensibility, which shows itself, under the action of excitants more or less intense, by pain and its expression, and by certain reflex symptoms whose immediate manifestation is spasm of the ducts.

3. These phenomena are especially determined by the presence and contact of foreign bodies (biliary calculi) whose spontaneous migration is, for that reason, rendered very difficult, and is not effected till after a variable time; and there is this peculiarity attending this migration, that these bodies may return to the gall bladder instead of passing downward to the intestine.

4. Anæsthetics and antispasmodics are best adapted to

Trousseau's penetrating mind understood this spasmodic action of the bile ducts. In the very faithful description which he has given in his Clinical Medicine* of hepatic colic, he speaks of the ejaculation of bile into the intestine, and assigns a considerable rôle to the muscular layer of these ducts. Senac, however, the author of a remarkable study on the treatment of hepatic colic published in 1870, has most clearly shown the importance of these spasms. Hence, from the point of view of general pathology, there is good warrant for placing the acute accidents determined by the passage of gall stones through the excretory ducts of the liver in the great group of colics, which, as

---

the treatment of this morbid state, of which it is easy to realize experimentally the mechanical conditions.

5. These medicaments, notably morphine, chloroform, hydrate of chloral, act by exercising an immediate anæsthetic and paralyzing influence, whence result the cessation of the spasmodic state, distention of the ducts, and the accumulation of bile, which acts upon the foreign body after the manner of a *vis à tergo* and forces it towards the intestine.

6. The association of hydrochlorate of morphine with chloroform or hydrate of chloral (*i. e.*, the simultaneous administration of these medicinal agents) constitutes the most powerful means for obtaining the results indicated. viz: anæsthesia of the bile ducts and consequent cessation of pain, and a favorable influence on the migration and rapid expulsion of the foreign bodies. (Laborde, Experimental Study on the Contractility, Spasm and Sensibility of the Bile Ducts. Bull. de Therap., 1873-74.

*Trousseau, Clirique Medicale de l Hôtel Dieu de Paris.

you know, are properly defined as the painful contractions of mucous tubes which have a muscular
layer.

Pardon me for dwelling so long upon these points,
but you will see that from a therapeutic standpoint
the recognition of the spasmodic element in hepatic
colic is of the utmost importance.

When a gall stone is formed, either it produces
no marked symptoms, as I have before said, or it gives
rise to two orders of phenomena, viz: the acute painful symptoms of hepatic colic, or, as is sometimes the
case, a train of obscure symptoms with slow evolution
and often of difficult diagnosis.

I can not here give you a lengthy description of
hepatic colic, and must refer you therefor to your
text books. I must however remind you that this affection, so rarely fatal, may be complicated with grave
accompaniments. Sometimes there is an inflammation of the bile ducts and gall bladder sufficiently intense to give rise to peritonitis of a more or less
spreading character; in other cases less well known
(and it is for this reason that I mention them), the
pain is so sever as to produce lipothymia and fatal
syncope.*

---

* Hepatic colic may be preceded by prodromes: vague
pains, cramps of the stomach, weight in the hepatic region;
but often it begins suddenly by a pain which appears with or
without appreciable cause, several hours after a meal. This
pain rapidly attains its maximum. It is atrocious, paroxysmal;

If hepatic colic in its ordinary form is quite easy of diagnosis, there are masked forms sufficiently common which often pass unperceived, and which at the same time by their symptoms indicate to the practiced eye the presence of biliary lithiasis. We have

---

it compels the patient to cry out. According to Durand-Fardel, the maximum of this pain is in the right hypochondriac region; according to Senac, on the contrary, it is in the epigastrium, and it is from this region that the pain radiates to the sides and posterior part of the body, to the vertebral column, to one or both shoulders, etc.

The patients are taken with extreme restlessness, they do not find any comfortable position in bed. There is one position to which Durand-Fardel cells attention, which they seem to prefer, viz: the sitting posture with the body bent forwards, the head resting on the knees.

At the beginning of the paroxysms, you sometimes observe a severe chill, epigastric distress, with vertigo, nausea, and vomiting, first of food then of bile; sometimes, also the patients may have convulsions, hysterical attacks, etc. Coincidently with the first attack, jaundice may appear; it is however sometimes wanting, especially in mild cases; it is variable both in intensity and extent, may remain limited to the sclerotics, to the circumference of the nose, or mouth, or may invade the whole body. During the entire attack, you observe little or no change in the pulse and temperature. Pressure over the liver is painful, and it is with difficulty that by palpation and percussion you can detect congestion of the organ.

After the attack, the patients suffer from general lassitude, which is in ratio of the intensity of the attack; there is often, also, want of appetite, nausea and vomiting; the bowels are always constipated; the urine is of a deep wine color, and contains the coloring matter of the bile.

cases where gastric symptoms predominate, and Senac has also done well in insisting upon this point; in fact the majority of patients affected with gall stones (sixty-five per cent.) suffer from painful cramps in the stomach. This variety of dyspepsia called *hepatic dyspepsia*, which I mentioned while on the treatment of affections of the stomach, has been studied by Cornillon, who has called attention to its frequency.*

---

* Fauconneau-Dufresne says also that we must refer to the accompaniments of lithiasis, many of the pains called *cramps of the stomach*, or regarded as spasmodic, neuralgic or rheumatic affections.

Willemin also indicates a prodromic period, constituted by dyspepsia, or gastric troubles recurring more or less often.

Senac has also noticed similar cases among persons sent to Vichy to be treated for "gastralgia" or "cramps of the stomach."

In some patients you have only these attacks of gastric cramp as a guide to diagnosis; in others, after the attack, you will notice that the urine is of a wine tint more or less marked; sometimes there is a jaundiced hue of the skin, which suffices to clear up the diagnosis.

Out of one hundred observations, Senac found sixty-five in which the only symptoms were of a gastric order:

Cramps of the stomach ....26 ⎱ 64	
Gastralgias ....20 ⎰	
Dyspepsia...	19
Pain in the epigastric region and in the back,............	3
Pain in the stomach and liver	3
Hepatic pains...	7
Sudden onset of the affection by well marked hepatic colic,	15
Cases where the existence or absence of prodromes was not mentioned.................................... ...	7
	100

To these gastralgic phenomena we may add another symptom quite as characteristic, namely, the appearance of remittent febrile attacks. Senac, who is so excellent authority on these subjects,* has shown that these intermittent attacks appear between four o'clock and six o'clock in the afternoon. They are accessions of little intensity, but in some cases, as Charcot has pointed out, they may take on the character of real pernicious paroxysms like those seen in the worst forms of malaria. We have here something very similar to what takes place in connection with states of the urinary passages when you catheterize certain individuals. You well know that febrile attacks of an intermittent character are often thereby provoked. It is the same with the bile ducts, where the presence of foreign bodies is the occasion of similar reflex symptoms.

I can affirm the reality of these facts; so whenever you have a patient with the symptoms of painful dyspepsia, in whom you observe a slight febrile movement coming on between four and five o'clock in the afternoon, especially if you notice a slight jaundiced hue which may be scarcely appreciable; moreover, if you find the region of the gall bladder sensitive and pain produced on pressure, you are warranted in affirming the presence of gall stones.

As you see, I have dwelt at some length on the pathogeny and symptoms of biliary lithiasis. I have

---

*Senac, Treatment of Hepatic Colic; 1870.

deemed it necessary to do so, because, before under-
taking the treatment, you should have mastered well
the first causes of the lithiasis and its accompaniments,
in order the more certainly and methodically to meet
them.

The treatment of biliary lithiasis should fulfil the
three following indications: To meet and allay the
symptoms determined by the presence of the calculus;
to attempt the solution of the latter, if this be possible;
lastly, to prevent their formation. Let us consider
the first indication, viz.: to combat the pain. This,
as before said, ordinarily takes the form of colic.
I shall not concern myself with those rare cases
which belong rather to the domain of surgery, and
which are connected with ulceration of the gall
bladder by the calculi and the passage of the latter
through the abdominal walls, and shall restrict myself
to the treatment of the colic itself.

But before proceeding any farther, we must settle
the question, Ought we to treat the colic at all ? I
have told you, in fact, that the reflex and painful
symptoms which characterize the colic are determined
by the passage of calculi through the bile ducts; this
passage is necessary; it is the only natural means of
getting rid of the trouble.

The attack of colic is then, as Durand-Fardel has
said, a necessary evil, and we ought not, properly
speaking, to treat the colic, if by the word *treat* we
are to understand *to oppose the passage of the calculus*

and its movements toward the intestine, which ought to be favored rather than hindered.

But we ought to render this transit as easy and painless as possible; and our duty is to relieve the suffering of the patient. To attain this result, there are four great therapeutic agents which we may employ: morphine,* chloral, chloroform and antipyrine.

Do not forget that one of the modes of introduction of medicaments, namely by the *primæ viæ*, is often denied us by reason of the continual vomiting of the patient, and that we are obliged, in order that our medicines may be absorbed and do good, to introduce them by the skin, the rectum, or the respiratory passages. Of these three channels the subcutaneous is the preferable one, and I recommend you to employ a combination of morphine and atropine, of which the following is a useful formula:

Ŗ Morphinæ hydrochloratis, 10 centigrams.
Atropinæ sulph., 1 centigram.
Cherry laurel water, 20 grammes.
M.

One cubic c. m. of this solution, or a hypodermic syringeful, contains ½ c. g. of morphine and ½ m. g. of atropine.

---

*A useful combination for hepatic colic is that known as chlorodyne or *chloranodyne* (P., D. & Co.), which contains chloroform and morphine. Dose, fifteen drops.—Tr.

This treatment is to-day very generally adopted, but there are those who object to it. Senac has shown himself one of the most determined opponents of these injections, and from what follows you will understand the grounds of his opposition.

In my experimental researches on spasm of the bile ducts, I had shown the reality of this spasm, and also explained the true mechanism of the colic; Laborde had confirmed these experiments, and our conclusion was a natural one, that morphine associated with atropine was the best remedial agent in our possession, as these alkaloids moderate the contraction of the smooth muscular fibres. But Senac, who had also taken up this idea of spasm, and was one of the first to put it in clear light, replied: " The contraction is necessary to the transit of the gall stone, and by your morphine injections you hinder the passage of the calculus into the intestine and thus you retard the cure of your patient."

Who is to be judge in this dispute? Clinical experience must decide. Never (and I emphasize the word *never*) in innumerable cases of hepatic colic have morphine injections appeared to prolong colic, and always practitioners have obtained from these injections relief of pain. The explanation seems simple enough. We recognize the fact that morphine, like atropine, opposes to a certain extent spasm of the unstriped fibres, but who will say that when this spasm exceeds certain limits, instead of favoring the passage of the calculus, it does not arrest it in its course by excess of contraction? However this may be, Senac has relaxed somewhat of his rigor, and to-day, like the greater number of physicians, he resorts to morphine injections in the most painful cases.

Before having recourse to injections of morphine, which are to be reserved for cases of great severity, in hepatic colic of medium intensity you may employ anodyne suppositories, of which the following is a good formula:

> ℞   Ext. belladonnæ, 1 centigramme.
>   Ext. opii, 2 centigrammes.
>   Olei theobrom., 3 grammes.
>   Ceræ albæ, q. s.
> M.—For one Suppository.

Chloral is also an excellent medicament when given in lavement according to the method which I advise, and which consists in dissolving two or three grammes in a cup of milk, in which the yolk of an egg has been beaten up, Unfortunately, chloral cannot render us great service. for, generally, patients under the tyranny of their colic cannot retain these injections.

Lastly, there is another means which I advise you to employ whenever, after injections of morphine, the pain still keeps its intensity. I cannot describe the agony of some typical cases of hepatic colic; you must be present yourself and witness this suffering, the incessant cries of the patient, the almost delirous agitation which nervous patients manifest. In these cases you may use chloroform by inhalation, following the method which obstetricians have popularized, and which has been called *obstetrical anæsthesia.* Administer the chloroform delicately, *i.e.,* pour ten, twenty or thirty drops upon a handkerchief, and let the patient inhale the anæsthetic; these inhalations you can repeat till you have obtained abatement of the pain with conservation of the intelligence. This, as you are aware, is Simpson's obstetric method; which has been also defended by Campbell. (*)

I have not spoken of the internal administration of chloroform, which Corlieu, a long time ago, extolled,(†) because administration by the stomach is very difficult, and because it is proved that this method is less efficacious than by the respiratory passages. I may say the same of the chloroform ointments in which some seem to have faith, but which hardly seem to me to have the merit of placebos.

However, as saturated chloroform water has been vaunted by some authorities, notably Lèsegue and Regnauld, you may employ this chloroform water for the intense pains in the stomach which individuals often suffer from who are victims of biliary lithiasis. Chloroform water is made by agitating a little chloro-

---

*Gaz. des Hop. 1856.

†Union Medicale, 1847.

form in pure water and allowing it to settle. The supernatant liquid which is decanted off contains a minute quantity of chloroform. If you administer chloroform water, you can prescribe it in the following way:

    ℞   Saturated chloroform water, 60 grams (2 f ℥).
        Orange flower water, 30 grams (1 f ℥).
        Syrup of poppy, 30 grams (1 f ℥).

    Sig.—A tablespoonful every quarter of an hour till the pains cease.

The analgesic properties of antipyrine have been applied by Germain See to the treatment of biliary lithiasis, and the professor has shown us the benefits which may be derived from it. I have myself often had recourse to antipyrine in bilious colic, and in certain cases I have obtained real service therefrom. You can employ the hypodermic or the rectal method. The hypodermic injections may be thus formulated:

    ℞   Antipyrine, grams v. -
        Water, grams xx.

    M. Sig. Inject a whole syringeful of this solution.

As these solutions are often painful, I prefer suppositories of antipyrine, or small rectal injections containing a gram of the medicament.

To these principal means you may add iced drinks and especially iced milk, warm baths, cataplasms over the hepatic region, and even the application of ice to the region of the liver.

So much for the treatment of hepatic colic. The attack yields at the end of several hours or of several days, according to circumstances, then disappears almost suddenly, and the patient finds the offending body in the stools. The diagnosis is settled; you know beyond doubt that the patient is affected with biliary lithiasis, and it is probable that he will again be afflicted in the same way.

Do we possess any means of preventing these recurrences, *i. e.*, is it possible to effect solution of those calculi which remain in the gall bladder ? In other words, is there a lithontriptic treatment of biliary calculus ? I believe we may reply categorically in the negative to this question, and at the same time, there is a certain number of remedies which are said to possess this property.

The most noted certainly is Durande's Solvent which consists of turpentine and sulphuric ether.

Jean Francois Durande who died in 1794 was physician and professor of Botany in this city (Paris). His formula for the solution of gall stones was as follows:

R Olei Terebinthinæ, 3 ij (8 grams),
Sulph. ether, 3 iij (12 grams.

M. Sig.—Half a teaspoonful to a teaspoonful in the morning, or night and morning.

This remedy is to be given in the morning along with glycerine or syrup, and washed down with a little whey or broth. The same dose may be repeated in the evening. Durande recommended to continue the usage of his specific till the patient had taken 5co grams (or about a pint); the medicine to be suspended, if irritation of the stomach should follow.

At the same time that he gave this preparation, Durande subjected his patient to a severe regimen with emollients and sometimes even practised blood letting.

Various modifications of Durande's formula have been proposed, thus, the proportion of turpentine has been augmented (2 parts turpentine to one of ether) or the proportion of ether has been augmented (2 parts ether to one of turpentine).

Turpentine is a very disagreeable remedy to take, and it is for this reason that its administration in capsules as Trousseau recommends, is preferable to the administration in emulsion: Trousseau's method was to give one capsule of turpentine and two of ether several times during the day.

Some have explained the action of the turpentine and ether mixture on the principle that gall stones in a capsule dissolve in such a menstruum. This chemical solution, however, is not as complete as you would suppose, but even admitting the chemical fact as true, it can not explain the results of the remedy when given internally. It is not to be supposed that these two substances when taken by mouth pass without transformation through the stomach and duodenum to reach the gall bladder by traversing the bile ducts, and there produce their solvent action. The explanation is then erroneous, and yet it must be admitted that this remedy has possessed and still possesses a great reputation based upon its clinical results, for there exist very many observations in which the employment of this means has attenuated and distanced the attacks of colic.

I do not believe that these favorable results imply the possibility of solution of the calculi, but they are doubtless due to the antispasmodic and calmative action of the ether and turpentine mixture, and not to any lithontriptic action. But however this may be, as the remedy easily fatigues the stomach, and as its antispasmodic properties are inferior to those of the other medicaments of which I have spoken, I think it is better to discard it altogether.

What I have said of Durande's "specific," I would apply also to the terebinthinate soap proposed by Franck (a mixture of sweet almond oil, turpentine, and caustic soda), to chloroform, counselled as a solvent by Corlieu, Bouchut and Gobley, and I say the same of the choleate of sodium recommended by Schiff, of the succinate of iron, the effects of which Buckler has vaunted, and, in general, of all those substances which have been considered as solvents of biliary calculi.*

---

* Corlieu was the first to counsel the employment of chloroform as a solvent of calculi. His formula is as follows:

> ℞ Chloroform, grams ij.
>   Alcohol, grams xvj.
>   Water, grams ccc.
> M.

Gobley has shown that cholesterine dissolves more rapidly in chloroform than in ether.

Cholagogues have also a considerable part in the treatment of biliary lithiasis; by favoring the flow of bile they oppose one of the frequent causes of the deposition of cholesterine, and as podophyllin is one of the most powerful cholagogues known, you will not be surprised that it has been recommended in these cases, As for myself, I much prefer euonymin, and to all my patients affected with biliary lithiasis, I order two of the following pills on going to bed:

Schiff considers that the precipitation of cholesterine is due to want of cholate of soda and potash in the bile. He therefore counsels the administration of two or three grains of cholate of soda thrice a day; the medicine to be continued until the economy is thoroughly under its influence, as is shown by irregularity of the pulse, which becomes very slow by rest, and markedly accelerated by the movements of the patient.

Buckler, of Baltimore, has advised chloroform, five drops every four hours, and the succinate of iron in the dose of a teaspoonful after each meal. He affirms that the succinate of iron has the power to dissolve cholesterine even in the blood, by setting free a considerable quantity of nascent oxygen. Buckler has affirmed that by this process he has rapidly obtained the solution of all the calculi that he has been called upon to treat.

Lothromp declares that for eighteen years he has treated with success more than twenty cases of biliary lithiasis with the succinate of iron alone.

Dabney (Am. Jour. Med. Sc., 1876,) also vaunts the employment of cholate of soda as a preventive of the formation of gall stones. He gives five grains twice a day.

Enonymin,
        Castile soap, ää 3 grammes (gr. xlv).
F. S. A. pil, No. xxx.

The really curative treatment of biliary lithiasis is the thermal treatment, *i. e.*, by the natural alkaline waters, and there are two spas especially whose waters are efficacious in these cases; I refer to Vichy and Carlsbad.

You remember that while speaking of chola-gogues, I mentioned the want of agreement which exists on this point between clinicians and physio-logists, and I have shown you how we must explain the undoubted curative action of these waters. Surely, it is not by dissolving the calculus that these waters act, but by ameliorating the digestive functions, by regulating nutrition, by diminishing the hepatic con-gestion which almost always accompanies the presence of calculi, lastly, by modifying the bile itself.

What differences exist between the waters of Carlsbad and Vichy, these two rival stations which possess an equal reputation acquired by innumer-able cures? It is chiefly owing to their richness in sodium bicarbonate that the waters of Vichy are efficacious. And it is chiefly to sodium sulphate that we are to look for the curative element in Carlsbad.*

---

*The Vichy Springs belong to Allier, a province in Central France. They are strongly alkaline; their temperature varies between 44° and 14° C.; their richness in sodium bicar-bonate is about 5 grammes per litre. There are 11 of these

Of the various Vichy waters, the Hôpital spring is the best for biliary lithiasis; the patient may drink a tumbler full four times a day. Of the Carlsbad waters, Sprudel is to be preferred. Add, that at this latter station the alimentary regimen is very severe, and at all the hotels patients are subjected to a uniform diet, which plays a considerable rôle in the treatment at these stations.*

---

springs, of which 4 are cold springs, the waters of which are fit for transportation.

We have no alkaline springs in this country comparable with these Vichy waters unless we except the Congress Springs, of California, which contain 2 grammes per litre of sodic bicarbonate; the Soda Springs of Wilhorts, Oregon, are also strongly alkaline. The Hathorn, Congress, High Rock, Vichy and other of the chloride of sodium waters of Saratoga, the St. Leon (Canada) are often prescribed for biliary lithiasis, and have proved useful in very many cases.

The Carlsbad waters (Carlsbad, Bohemia), are the type of sodic sulphate waters. There are 10 principal springs, of which the most important is Sprudel. There are in every litre over 2 grammes sulphate of sodium, and 3 of carbonates of sodium, magnesium and potassium. The taste of the Sprudel water is salty, brackish and strongly alkaline. From two to three glasses are usually drank per day. These Carlsbad waters are alterative and laxative, and have a great reputation in Europe for biliary lithiasis.—TRANS.

*The Sprudel water gives a sensation of comfort and even of hilarity after drinking it. When taken in quantities not exceeding half a tumblerful, it has little effect, but it becomes purgative after drinking from three to six glasses. This water also produces nervous disturbances of a very curious nature,

Whether they act by the bicarbonate or sulphate of sodium which they contain, the waters of Vichy and Carlsbad produce essentially the same effect; *i. e.*, patients experience almost always during the employ of these waters, or, as is most frequently the case, one or two months afterward, new attacks of colic, due to the passing of the calculi. But this is a necessary evil, as I have before shown you, and it is essential that for a period of years the patient shall periodically resort to these waters in order to get completely rid of the biliary lithiasis which causes the calculi.

Other thermal stations have also been recommended, bnt they occupy a second rank in the treatment of biliary lithiasis. I refer to Vittel, Contrexiville, Niederbronn, and Capvern. The sodium sulphate waters ought all to enter into this group of lithontriptic waters, and we must place at the head of these waters, not the Hunyadi Janos, which contains sulphate of magnesia, a salt which is but slightly cholagogue, but the Rubinat water, which contains sulphate of sodium in larger proportion than almost any other mineral water.

After the employment of mineral waters, we must

which may be compared to drunkenness; vertigo, dazzling sensations, loss of memory, etc.

By evaporating Sprudel water, a salt is obtained very much in use in Germany as a purgative, and known as Carlsbad salt; the composition is almost exclusively sodium sulphate. Sprudel water contains 2.27 grammes of this salt per litre.

assign the first importance to hygiene in the means at our disposal for the cure of lithiasis. The hygienic regimen should be absolutely based on the different physiological circumstances which, as I showed you at the beginning of this lecture, modify the excretion of bile. Cholesterine, as I have told you, is a product of the disassimilation of the nervous system; urge your patients then to avoid too intense mental emotions and everything that can cause undue exercise of the cerebro-spinal axis.

We must, as I have before said, guard against stasis of the bile in the gall bladder. Recommend then exercise, active respiratory movements, which have for their effect both to oxidize fatty matters and hydrocarbons, and to exert pressure on the gall bladder. Catarrh of the bile ducts, through the mucus which it engenders, may be the commencement of biliary calculi; counsel, then, avoidance of all the producing causes of catarrh and, and for this end forbid too highly seasoned foods, too generous wines, and too abundant meals.

Lastly, from the point of view of diet, without absolutely forbidding fatty foods, I would advise a very moderate use of fats, and urge you above all to insist upon a vegetable rather than an animal diet, for it seems to be demonstrated that it is the acidity of the bile which most favors the precipitation of cholesterine, and this acidity may be produced by a diet largely nitrogenous; but you should be very chary in the permission of starches and sugars, and ever keep before you the excellent precepts given by that master in dietetics, Prof. Bouchardat, as well as the therapeutic indications which have so recently been formulated by Prof. Bouchard.

Bouchardat's alimentary regimen for biliary lithiasis is as follows:

Eat moderately, abstain from soups containing sorrel, tomatoes, etc., and from strong liquors; regulate the employment of tea and coffee according to their effects. One egg and never more during the day, or entire abstinence from eggs. Meats of all kinds (butcher's meat, fowl, game) may be permitted, but must be used with moderation.

It is necessary to be still more reserved in respect to fish, lobsters, cray fishes and crabs, shrimps, and other shell fishes, as well as old cheese. Milk and fresh cheese are unobjectionable. The vegetables and legumes of the season are almost all indicated, and should be a part of every day's fare. I would particularize spinach, lettuce, chiccory, artichokes, cucumbers, carrots, parsnips, sweet potatoes, asparagus, green beans and peas in moderate quantity.

Potatoes are useful and should in part replace bread at meals; bread, in fact, ought to be eaten moderately, and the crust is preferable to the rest of the loaf. Common radishes and black radishes may be eaten freely, also cabbages, cauliflowers, Brussels cabbage, mushrooms, truffles, chestnuts and other nuts; beans and lentils in moderate quantity are permitted.

The daily use of water cresses or of salads, lettuce, endives, chiccory, Indian cresses, dandelion, corn-salad, viper's grass, etc., is allowable.

All the fruits may be freely eaten (raspberries, peaches, bananas, strawberries, prunes, figs, etc.) The "grape cure" is often beneficial. Olives, almonds, pistachio nuts, etc., in moderate quantity. Little or no beer; the only alcoholic beverage, red or white wine with twice or three times as much water. The sparkling wines are contra-indicated, as well as the effervescing waters.

For constipation, Bouchardat recommends to be taken in the morning in sweetened lemonade, a tablespoonful of a mixture of equal parts of Rochelle salts and Glauber salts. The healthy function of the skin should be promoted by a sponge bath in the morning, followed by a brisk rub-down with a dry towel or flesh brush, or the naked hand, oiled with a little sweet oil. Once or twice a week, a hygienic alkaline bath (three ounces carbonated potash, half a drachm of essence of lavender, a drachm and a half of compound tincture of benzoin to the water of the bath). These baths to be followed by prolonged rubbing and massage.

Lastly, to prevent the formation of calculi, take for the first ten days of the month, morning and evening before meals, a pill containing a grain and a half of tartrate of potassa and lithia; each pill to be washed down with a tumbler of water. For the ten following days, morning and evening, a table-spoonful of a mixture containing the syrup of five roots with a little acetate of potassium. [May be replaced in American practice by the syrup of buckthorn, or the cascara cordial to which acetate of potassium may be added.] For the ten succeeding days of the month, a quart of water every day containing in solution a couple drachms of Rochelle salts.

In the spring, the patient may take to advantage every morning on rising, four ounces of the juice of herbs (lettuce, chiccory, dandelion), with 75 grains of acetate of potash. This to be followed up for a month.

According to Bouchard, the pathogenetic conditions of the production of gall stones are as follows: 1, Excess of cholesterine; 2, Lack of fatty acids; 3, Lack of biliary acids; 4, Lack of alkaline bases; 5, Excess of acids in the organism; 6, Lime in solution in the organism.

These unfavorable conditions may depend on the diet, on digestion. on the hepatic function, on general nutrition, and on respiration.

In respect to diet. we should exclude brains, blood puddings, and the yolk of egg. The ternary aliments should be used with extreme moderation, and fats should be preferred to sweets and starches; farinaceous substances should enter as a very small part into the diet, as well as leguminous substances, being too rich in starch and in lime. Green vegetables and fruits may be sparingly indulged in, notwithstanding the lime and vegetable acids which they contain, sweet effervescent drinks, and especially the sparkling wines, beer, cider, etc., are to be interdicted, but red wine and coffee may be permitted. Hard drinking waters are to be avoided; in fact, the purer the drinking water the better.

To favor the biliary secretion, the sodic chloride or sodic sulphate or magnesia sulphate waters are to be recommended (Blue Lick, Lansing, St. Leon, Saratoga and Ballston waters, Freidrichshall, Hombourg, Kissingen, Marienbad, Brides, Pullna, etc.). It is a good plan to send patients to the warm springs of Vichy, or, better still, to Carlsbad.

To promote the general nutrition, you should have recourse to all the great stimulants of the nervous system which energize the metamorphoses of the economy. Recommend frictions of the skin, cold affusions, warm salt baths, cold sea baths, exercise in the open air, sea air, mountain air, corporal exercise to be taken fasting and several hours after meals. (Bouchardat on the Hygienic Treatment of Biliary Lithiasis, (Bull. de Thérap., t. xcix, p. 145). Bouchard, Maladies par ralentissement de la nutrition, Paris, 1882, p. 102).

Along with the purely medical treatment I must allude to the surgical treatment of biliary lithiasis. Emboldened by the success attained by antiseptic

methods in operations practiced upon the peritoneum,
certain physicians have proposed to open the gall
bladder for biliary obstruction. When the gall bladder is distended by large calculi, and the outflow of
bile is thereby hindered, these surgeons, following the
lead of Godefroy Muller who performed cholecystotomy about the middle of the last century, have advised to cut into the gall bladder, and remove stones
contained in this sac.

Cholecystotomy has been performed by Lawson
Tait, of England, by Bernays, of St. Louis, by Parkes,
of Chicago, by Langenbrich, of Berlin, by Musser
and Keen, of Philadelphia, etc.

Some have gone even farther in this direction,
and have proposed completely to extirpate the gall
bladder and to substitute cholecystectomy for cholecystotomy.

The future must decide as to the practicability
and safety of such surgical interference. It must
however be admitted that a great number of surgeons of our country are becoming every day more
strenuous advocates of cholecystotomy.

Cholecystotomy was practiced about the middle of the
last century by Godefroy Müller, who opened up a biliary
fistula, and following it to the gall bladder, broke up a calculus and removed it by piecemeal. Afterwards the operation went into oblivion. Since the progress of the antiseptic
method, there has been a revival of interest in cholecystotomy, and recently Drs. Musser and W. W. Keen, of Philadelphia, have compiled thirty-five cases in which this opera-

tion has been performed, in twenty-five of which it was successful.

In cases of biliary lithiasis with perceptible swelling of the gall bladder, two kinds of operations have been proposed; the incision of the gall bladder and removal of the calculus, or complete extirpation of the gall bladder. Before proceeding to either of these operations, it is necessary to confirm the diagnosis by suitable exploratory methods.

Aspiration is often innocuous, but it may give rise to accidents such as hæmorrhages or local peritonitis. Through the aspirating needle it is possible to pass a fine probe by which to percuss the calculi. But, according to Keen, the most certain result is furnished by acupunctures. With small steel needles, you may perforate the gall bladder with safety, and determine the presence or absence of calculi.

Lastly, the exploratory incision, ordinarily harmless when it is practised with antiseptic precautions, is the best means of detecting calculi in the gall bladder, while enabling you to complete the operation at the same sitting, if the gall bladder be found to contain stones.

The different stages of the operation have been carefully mapped out.

The incision is made over the centre of the tumor horizontally with the lower border of the ribs. It must be large enough to enable the operator to explore the deep parts. The knife should be carried to either side as far as may be necessary. All oozing of blood must be stopped before opening the peritoneum. The latter having been penetrated by an opening large enough to admit the finger and even the hand if necessary, the exploration of the gall bladder, of the cystic duct, and of the neighboring parts is made with care. If impacted gall stones are found, the gall bladder is opened, emptied of its calculi, and a biliary fistula is established by attaching the opening in the bladder to the lips of the abdominal wound. The fistula gets well in a few days.

The gall bladder has also been removed, but the dissection is difficult, gives rise to hæmorrhage, and is much the more dangerous operation.*

Pardon me, gentlemen, for having so long dwelt on the treatment of biliary lithiasis, but this is a disease of the liver very common in our climate and one which you will often be called upon to treat, and I trust I have given you hints which will be of use to you in your practice.

---

*Articles by Drs. Keen and Musser in the American Journal of Medical Sciences, October, 1884, and Braithwaite's Retrospect, Part 91, page 249. See also Medical Record, Vol. xxvii, page 499, and Vol. xxviii, page 716. Brun has summed up the observations down to the date of his writing in an article in the Archives Générales de Médécine, January, 1885.

CHAPTER IV.

TREATMENT OF JAUNDICE.

SUMMARY.—Symptoms of Jaundice, Causes—Jaundice by Obstruction—Spasmodic Jaundice—Pathological Physiology
of Jaundice by Obstruction—Treatment of Catarrhal
Jaundice—Hygienic Treatment—Medical Treatment—
Symptoms of Acholia—Jaundice without Obstruction—
Pathological Physiology of Jaundice without Obstruction
—Therapeutic Indications—Grave Jaundice—Pathological Physiology of Grave Jaundice—Therapeutic Indications.

GENTLEMEN:—In the previous lecture I alluded
to a symptom which almost always accompanies biliary
lithiasis, viz.: jaundice. I have reserved the consideration of this symptom, so common in affections of
the liver, for the present lecture, and shall now study
the subject at some length, with the therapeutic indications pertaining thereto.

You know that jaundice is characterized by the
passage of bilirubin in the blood and in the different
humors of the economy; you know also that besides
the yellowish color of the integument and conjunctivæ,
which is the result of the impregnation of the blood
by this principle, you find in the urine a sure and precise means of diagnosis by detecting there the presence of bilirubin. One of the most certain tests is the
action of nitrous nitric acid, and the multiplicity of
colors which it causes; another is the emerald green

tint obtained by tincture of iodine, or the azotite (nitrite) of potash.*

When you take a general survey of the pathogeny of icterus considered as a symptom of hepatic affections, you find that this symptom sometimes accompanies obstacles to the excretion of the bile; sometimes, on the contrary, these obstacles do not exist, and the bile flows freely into the intestine, but jaundice none the less ensues; lastly, sometimes the jaundice is

---

* Jaundiced urine is of a more or less deep greenish-yellow color, and stains linen. As a test for bilirubin, the nitrous nitric acid test is the best. Filter a little of the urine, and from a pipette, let fall a few drops of this acid (nitric, with a little nitrous) on a small quantity of the filtered urine in a test-tube. You observe a play of colors: green, blue, violet, red and yellow.

In doubtful cases, you can employ the following means: Agitate a little of the urine with hot chloroform, which dis- solves bilirubin, then pour off the chloroform, filter and drop in a little nitric acid which floats upon the chloroform; the play of colors is produced if there be bilirubin present.

The tincture of iodine test is applied in this manner: Filter a little of the urine and add a few drops of tincture of iodine. A beautiful emerald green color is produced.

Heller proposes this test for doubtful cases: He adds a little albumen to the urine, then drops in the HNO_3 which gives to the albumen the play of colors previously described.

Pettenkofer's test for the bile acids is the addition of a little strong H_2SO_4, drop by drop to a small quantity of the urine to which sugar has been added (one part sugar to four parts urine). The mixture is stirred with a glass rod, and first takes on a violet then a purple-red color.

attended with severe and speedily fatal symptoms and constitutes, both by its own violence and the complications which it determines, a disease of the utmost gravity.

Hence we have three great divisions of jaundice, each of which demands different treatment; icterus without obstruction, icterus with obstruction, and grave icterus.

But, do you ask me now, from a clinical point of view, how can we recognize these three varieties of jaundice? Nothing is more simple. In patients affected with jaundice, the fæcal matters either contain bile and are colored, or they contain no bile and are colorless.

In the latter case you have to do with icterus with obstruction, and in the former with icterus without obstruction. Does a case of jaundice present itself with a train of symptoms bespeaking a state of general constitutional infection? *i. e.*, with nervous, febrile or grave adynamic disturbances? You have before you, either a case of grave primary icterus, or a case of "aggravated" icterus, a variety of grave icterus belonging properly to the terminal period of several attacks of hepatitis. Hence, as you see, nothing is easier than this diagnosis when once you have detected the passage of bilirubin into the blood and urine. It suffices to examine the stools and general symptoms to determine the kind of jaundice.

Let us then examine the first of these groups, *i. e.*,

icterus by obstruction: the causes are subdivided into three groups. In the first group, the cause resides within the bile ducts themselves, as in biliary lithiasis, where the calculi obstruct more or less completely the excretory conduits, and determine an icterus which may be temporary or persistent.

Besides biliary calculi, authors have also admitted an icterus caused by obstruction of the ducts, due to thickened bile (Murchison and Frerichs); to foreign bodies (Saunders); to lumbrici, to hydatids, to distomata.

Jaundice may also be caused by a congenital absence or obliteration of the duct (fatal icterus of new born children); by a swelling of the bile ducts, due to perihepatitis; by an obliteration of the orifice of the choledochus by reason of an ulcer of the duodenum (Murchison); by cicatrices resulting from ulcers caused by presence of calculi, etc. Tumors within the bile duct may also cause obstruction, but ordinarily the compression comes from tumors in the vicinity—tumors of the liver, cancers, hydatids, hypertrophied lymphatic glands, tumors of the stomach, of the pancreas, of the kidneys, etc., aneurisms, (Frerichs), the gravid uterus compressing the common bile duct, and ovarian or uterine tumors.

In the second group, the cause of the icterus is in the walls of the bile ducts, as in catarrhal icterus, where the jaundice is determined by inflammation of the ductus choledochus, which produces swelling of the mucosa and the formation of mucus plugs which oppose the passage of the bile.

It is in the same group that authorities would place the so-called spasmodic icterus, *i. e.*, icterus determined by contraction of the muscular tunic of

the bile ducts, said to be at times sufficiently intense
to prevent the excretion of the bile. But I utterly
deny the existence of this spasmodic icterus, and although I fully believe in the possibility of spasm of
the choledochus duct, my experiments have shown
that this spasmodic action is never intense enough or
persistent enough to be the cause of anything like
prolonged arrest of the passage of the bile.

Lastly, in the third group of jaundice by obstruction the cause of the jaundice resides outside of the
bile ducts. We have, in fact, to do with all kinds of
tumors compressing these ducts and thus opposing the
outflow of bile.

I have just stated that whenever, from any cause,
the bile does not flow into the intestine, jaundice appears.

There are several explanations of this fact. Some
believe that the biliary secretion is suppressed by
virtue of the obstruction. The liver, they say, simply
separates the bile from the blood, and when this sep-
aration does not take place, the bile accumulates in
the blood and causes symptoms of jaundice. This
theory, which is called the functional theory, is similar
to that which is invoked in explanation of the uræmia
which supervenes when the ureters are tied in an
animal. But this interpretation which is quite applicable to the kidney, is not applicable to the liver,
because, as I have already told you in the previous
lecture, the hepatic gland does not simply separate the

materials of the bile from the blood, but forms *de novo* from that fluid the principal elements of this secretion.

The second explanation is more physiological. It affirms that the bile when it accumulates in the excretory ducts is absorbed and passes back into the blood. The experiments of Heidenhain, and especially of Picard, of Lyons, have in fact shown that very active absorption goes on in the mucous membrane of the bile ducts. I believe, then, that this latter theory, called theory of resorption, is the only one which explains the facts now before us.

But with what rapidity does this absorption of bile take place. The experiments which Audigé and myself have undertaken have convinced us that the passage of bilirubin into the circulation is more rapid than is generally supposed.

We have, in fact, shown that when you tie the common bile duct in a dog, and examine the urine, it is four hours after the ligature before the first traces of bilirubin appear in that excretion.

This was the view which Saunders defended in 1795, but which has been in our time combated by Frerichs, who affirms that the passage of bile into the urine does not take place until at the end of from 18 to 30 hours.*

_____

* Frerichs, Treatise on Diseases of the Liver; Saunders, Treatise on the Liver; Dujardin-Beaumetz and Audigé, loc. cit.

Wickham Legg has made some experiments on cats in which he practised ligature of the bile ducts. He affirms

What are the therapeutic indications in icterus by obstruction?

First, remove the obstacle if it be possible, and favor the flow of bile, then combat the symptoms which are due to this obstruction. To fulfil the first indication, we have already seen what must be done when the obstacle is a gall stone.

What now should be the treatment when the obstacle is a mucous plug. In other words, what is the treatment of that most common form of jaundice, catarrhal jaundice? This jaundice, bear in mind, is the result of an inflammation of the bile ducts, an inflammation which is generally secondary, and the consequence of an irritation of the upper part of the intestine (the duodenum). This mucous plug which obliterates the biliary conduits and thus explains the catarrhal jaundice, is not a matter of theory, a mere assumption, and Vulpian has demonstrated its undoubted existence in animals. How will you treat

---

that in this animal the icteric hue of the conjunctiva appears but tardily. Most of the animals died in from two to twenty-nine days after ligature of the ducts. Two of the surviving animals were killed from twenty-seven to twenty-nine days after the operation, but in these cases the ducts were found not to be absolutely impervious, some bile still filtering through into the duodenum despite the ligature. In all these observations there was a notable augmentation of the connective tissue of the liver, although the hepatic cells seemed to be intact.*

*Wickham Legg, on "The Changes in the Liver which follow Ligature of the Bile Ducts," St. Bartholomew's Hospital Reports, 1873, page 161.

this cholecystitis? By hygienic means, on the one hand, and therapeutic means on the other.

The hygienic means pertain principally to the dietary, and especially to milk diet. In fact, this gastro-duodenitis, which has brought about by contiguity and continuity of morbid action the cholecystitis, is generally the result of a too excitant or too abundant diet.

Our duty in these cases is to let the organ rest, but as this means if fully carried out is incompatible with life, you should advise the kind of food which is the least irritating. Recommend, then, to your patients to employ a milk diet exclusively. You may add alkalies and alkaline waters, which regulate the functions of nutrition, calm irritation of the primæ viæ, and favorably modify the hepatic circulation.

Then, again, you should stimulate the biliary secretion, in order to endeavor to overcome the obstacle causing the jaundice. You may give podophyllin, euonymin, or calomel, drawing largely from the group of cholagogues of which I gave you a description in a former lecture. You will especially employ those which have a manifest purgative action, and for this reason, that the intestinal acholia, which is the result of the obliteration of the bile ducts, always entails more or less obstinate constipation.

Make use, then, of the saline purgatives with a sodium sulphate basis, or the mineral waters, such as Carlsbad and Rubinat, which owe their activity principally to this salt. Employ also an excellent method prescribed by Krull, *i. e.*, give to your patient twice a day a large enema of cold water. You know that Vulpian has shown that in animals these irrigations of cold water have a powerful cholagogue action.*

Such are the most common and useful therapeutic measures in this affection; by their use the catarrhal jaundice may disappear quite promptly, but in other cases it is more persistent and may last for months. It will be necessary then to have recourse to other means which fulfil the second indication mentioned, viz.: to combat the symptoms caused by the passage of bilirubin into the blood. This therapeutic indication is especially applicable to persistent and chronic icterus, which manifests itself constantly by such symptoms as these: there is obstinate constipation, but this is not all—the intestinal acholia also prevents regular absorption from the surface of the intestine. Recall to mind what I told you, when lecturing on diseases of the intestines, respecting the utility of bile from a digestive point of view. Bile excites the peristaltic movements and clears the bowel, neutralizes the acidity of substances peptonized by the stomach,

---

* Krull recommends to slowly inject, by the Davidson's or fountain syringe, from one to two quarts of water, temperature about 50° F. The patient should keep up the injection as long as possible. (Krull On the treatment of catarrhal jaundice by rectal injections of cold water, Bull. de Therap., t. XC, iii, p. 212).

and, to a certain extent, opposes the fermentation of matters contained in the intestine, and perhaps favors the digestion of fatty substances. Hence the phenomena which have been noticed in jaundice by obstruction: retardation in the functions of nutrition, bleaching of the fecal matters, which often have a horribly fœtid odor. Such are the symptoms produced by acholia.

We must endeavor, as far as possible, to antagonize these bad effects. We must give purgatives, we must administer food in little quantity and such as demands but little work on the part of the intestine, we must also take care that what the patient eats shall not give rise to too active a fermentation in the intestine; and the most of these indications, it must be admitted, are met by an aliment whose utility I cannot too much extol, viz: milk.

You want especially to combat here the symptoms arising from intestinal putridity, which result from absence of bile in the intestine; bile being, as I have told you, an antiseptic agent of the first order. For my part, I am persuaded that in explaining the nervous symptoms which ensue in prolonged cases of jaundice, we should make much account of the penetration into the economy of putrid substances and of ptomaines absorbed from the surface of the intestine.

Many means have been advised. Some have proposed wood charcoal, others iodoform, others, as Bouchard, naphthalin or naphthol; for my part, I recommend you to employ sulphide of carbon water, of which I have often spoken to you before, and whose formula is as follows:

R Pure sulphide of carbon, 25 grams.
Water, 500 grams.
Essence of peppermint, 30 gtt.

M.—Place in a flask capable of holding 700 cubic centimetres. Shake the mixture and allow it to settle. Decant off the clear solution when needed. Renew the water as fast as it is poured off from the flask. You may give every day five or six tablespoonfuls of this carbon bisulphide water, taking care to dilute each dose in half a tumbler of milk.

In employing this simple remedy, you will see the fœtidity of the stools rapidly disappear in the most intense cases of jaundice by retention.

Bilirubin produces very painful cutaneous itching. I have known patients in whom this symptom became a veritable torture, and you must expect to witness this pruritus at advanced periods of icterus. What succeeds best in these cases is massage and vapor baths, which temporarily allay this annoying pruritus.

Lastly, bilirubin, in being absorbed into the blood, determines phenomena very similar to those caused by digitalis, i. e. it slows the pulse and circulation. Icterus even modifies the state of the heart muscle, and gives rise to a cardiac murmur which has been studied especially by Potin, Gangolphe, Morel, Fabre, Tessier, of Lyons, etc. Moreover, it alters the blood

8 x

crasis and gives rise to hemorrhages, of which Monneret has treated at length. It produces also in the
mental functions a very peculiar modification to which
alienists have called attention, which manifests itself
principally by hypochondriasis and profound gloom.*

---

* Frerichs, in the case of icterus has seen the pulse fall
28 or more beats. Besides the slowing of the pulse a disturbance of the heart rhythm has been noted, and this disturbance has been known to last for several weeks. This slowing
of the pulse had been before noted by Bouchard. Rohrig,
Feltz, and Ritter have shown that the injection of bile and in
particular of the biliary acids, into the blood immediately produces slowing of the pulse and heart.

The study of the alterations of the heart produced under
the influence of icterus is of quite recent date. These alterations
manifest themselves by a *bruit de souffle* whose origin is not yet
well known. * * * This peculiar mitral murmur is accompanied by a presystolic *bruit de galop*. According to Fabre,
there are three kinds of cardiac troubles in icterus; troubles in
the innervation of the heart, troubles in the nutrition of the
left ventricle, and dilatation of the right ventricle.

As for the intimate mechanism of this cardiac change, it is
very obscure. Morel, of Lyons, maintains that these disorders
depend on an elevation of tension in the cardio-pulmonary
system, whose mediate cause is an excitation of the sympathetic
filaments of the abdominal viscera, an excitation first con-
veyed to the bulbus, then reflected upon the cardio-pulmonary
organs.(a)

(a) Louis Gangolphe, On the mitral bruit de souffle in Icterus,
Thèse de Paris, 1875; Morel, Experimental Researches on the Pathology
of Lesions of the Right Heart consecutive to certain principal diseases of
the Liver and Intestines, Thèse de Paris, 1880; Laurent, Modifications of
the Heart-sounds in Cirrhosis of the Liver, Thèse de Paris, 1880; Fabre,
Fragments of Clinical Medicine, 1881, p. 194.

How are you to treat these symptoms ? Principally by favoring as far as possible the elimination of
bilirubin from the blood, and in seeking to accomplish
this you will have to avail yourself of the two great
emunctories the kidneys and lungs.

Respiration has an important office in the combustion of the coloring matter of the bile, which belongs to the group of carbon compounds, and Frerichs
has rightly insisted on the utility of compelling the
patient to live out of doors, take long walks and in-
dulge in gymnastic exercises.

The kidneys play an important part in the elimination of bilirubin, and we find constantly in the urine
of jaundiced patients a considerable quantity of this
coloring principle. You must, then, promote the
elimination of this substance, and you will see, when I
come to speak of grave icterus, that if, for any reason,
this emunctory becomes obliterated in the icteric,
accidents of high gravity supervene. Therefore, I am
fully of the opinion of Decaudin * respecting the
functions of the kidneys in jaundice, and ascribe to
that organ an important rôle in the production of
malign icterus. You ought then, in chronic icterus,

---

* Thése de Paris, 1878.

The alterations of the kidneys in jaundice have been but
recently studied. Vogel, Kölliker and Leyden, have shown
how variable is the quantity of urine excreted in 24 hours by
the icteric. Wickham Legg affirms that ligature of the bile
ducts is accompanied with polyluria; Feltz and Buckler have

to administer diuretics and especially milk, that admirable medicament, which, fulfilling special indications pertaining to digestion, also assists the elimination of bilirubin by the urine.

Support also the forces of the patient, do what you can to prevent hemorrhages; oppose the evils resulting from retardation of the circulation, by subjecting your patient to a tonic treatment of which quinine shall be an important element. Prescribe journeyings and change of scene; you will thus divert your patient's mind from constant brooding over his disease, and thus antagonize the gloom and depression of spirits so common to icteric patients.

Under the influence of persistent obliteration of the bile ducts, there is produced, at first, an abnormal dilatation of the biliary net work and of the gall bladder, then, secondary alterations of the liver, veritable scleroses, well described by Prof. Charcot, which we shall study more fully when we come to the subject of hypertrophic sclerosis. Two therapeutic means have been proposed for this dilatation of the biliary passages and gall bladder—aspiration or paracentesis of

shown that the injection of bilirubin into the blood has the same effect.

When the icterus is prolonged, there sometimes takes place in the renal ducts a deposition of pigment which alters the epithelium, and gives rise to pigment cylinders in the urine, which have been observed by Budd, Johnson, Virchow, Nothnagel and Gubler.

the gall bladder, and electrization, according to the method of Gerhardt, of Wurzbourg.*

Such are the therapeutics of icterus with obstruction, and although this treatment seems simple, precise, and adapted to the different indications which re-

---

* The alterations of structure consecutive to ligature of the common bile duct have been studied by Wickham-Legg, Charcot, Gombault and Chambard. They are characterized by the following signs: the perilobular ducts begin first to dilate, then there is an inflammation around these canaliculi, and this peri-angiocholitis leads to the production of connective tissue fibres constituting a veritable experimental sclerosis, which Charcot describes under the name of *insular* and *uni-lobular sclerosis.*

Ducastel pointed out this kind of peri angio-cholitis in a case of biliary calculus which was lodged in the ductus choledochus. (W. Legg, in St. Bartholomew's Hospital Report vol. xii, p. 23: Charcot and Gombault in Arch. de Phys., 1876, etc.)

In a patient of his affected with obliteration of the common bile duct, Dixon (Practitioner, April, 1876,) aspirated the gall bladder and drew off on five separate occasions a few grammes of bile; each aspiration was attended with great re-relief.

As for electrization of the gall bladder in catarrhal jaunice, Gerhardt's method is of the simplest kind. He employs a strong faradic current. One pole is applied as accurately as possible with some pressure (the place being determined by palpation and percussion) over the region of the gall-bladder. The other pole is placed on the region of the back opposite, and now and then both poles are moved to and fro. Gerhardt claims remarkable results (even the overcoming of mucous obstruction and reduction of the gall bladder) from this Faradic treatment. (Gerhardt, in Berlin Klin. Woch., 1873, No. 47.)

sult from suppression of the biliary secretion, do not forget that icteric patients are difficult patients to treat. This yellow discoloration of the integument frightens the patient and his family; so when the affection lasts for some time, you will need to resort to all the means which I have pointed out, in order to vary the treatment and allay the impatience of the patient.

The precision of therapeutic indications which characterizes the kind of jaundice just described is wanting when we come to the study of icterus without obstruction, and the difficulty here results chiefly from the uncertainty in which we find ourselves regarding the pathogeny of these kinds of jaundice. This very fact, gentlemen, shows us that our therapeutic system should always be based on solid physiological and clinical data, for when these bases are wanting, as in icterus without obstruction, our therapeutic indications become hesitating.

Jaundice without obstruction supervenes despite the excretion of bile, and often even when the bile is secreted too abundantly.

According to Murchison, jaundice without obstruction may be referred to one of the causes enumerated below:

1. Presence in the blood of poisons which oppose the normal metamorphoses of the bile.

2. Enfeeblement or disorder of the innervation controlling these metamorphoses.

3. Insufficient oxygenation of the blood, which has the same result.

4. Hypersecretion of the bile, more being absorbed than can be transformed in the normal state.

5. Abnormal retention of bile in the bile ducts and intestines by reason of habitual or prolonged constipation.

I shall endeavor as far as possible to bring into agreement clinical experience and the different theories which have been broached to explain this icterus. Writers have hypothecated modifications of the blood in explanation of this kind of jaundice, or have assumed troubles in the biliary secretion, and others still, perturbations taking place in the functions of the liver.

Those who have ascribed icterus without obstruction to alterations in the blood, support one of two theories, the one advocated by Frerichs, the other by Kuhne.

According to the teachings of Frerichs, the bile which flows into the intestine passes in the normal state back into the blood, where the biliary acids are transformed into the coloring matter of the bile; then this coloring matter is burned and destroyed as fast as produced. But let any circumstance oppose this oxidation, and the bilirubin, being no longer burned, passes into the blood and the different humors of the economy.

According to this theory, the failure of oxidation is the cause of this hæmatogenous icterus, which it will not do to confound with hæmaphæic icterus, and you understand why it is that Murchison has made of this a special group under the name of icterus by insufficient oxygenation of the blood.*

According to Kuhne, whose explanation starts from similar data, the bile which passes into the intestine under normal conditions is reabsorbed into the blood, where the biliary acids (as seems demonstrated by experimentation) destroy the globules and set at liberty the hæmoglobin which is transformed into bilirubin. When the transformation is too active, naturally the bilirubin would accumulate in the blood and produce jaundice.

Other physiologists regard this jaundice as simply and solely due to resorption of bile from the surface of the intestine. I have already shown you that Lussana and Schiff ascribe a great importance to this "entero-hepatic circulation," which they say goes on between the intestine and the liver. The bile poured into the intestine is reabsorbed by the portal circulation, and returns to the liver, to be anew excreted into the intestine. It is easy to understand that when the biliary secretion is too abundant, a certain quantity of bile and coloring matter may pass into the blood and produce jaundice. Vulpian† has, in fact, shown, in contradiction to the experiments of Feltz and Ritter,

---

* The icterus of the newly-born, according to Murchison, comes under this category, so also many cases of icterus in acute pneumonia.

† Vulpian, Course of Lectures on the Liver, École de Médécine.

that when bile is injected into the veins of animals
jaundice is produced.

Lastly, other physiologists have maintained that it
is in the liver itself that we are to look for the cause
of jaundice without obstruction, and in certain pathological circumstances the bile which is secreted in the
hepatic cells may pass, not into the radicles of the bile
ducts which surround them, but directly into the net-
work of blood-vessels with which the liver is so richly
endowed.

Which of these theories shall we adopt? Is there
any one which responds better than the others to the
different facts which clinical experience furnishes?
No, all the theories which I have enumerated may
find their application in individual cases belonging to
the large group of icterus without obstruction.

Jaundice with polycholia, in which congestion
of the liver entails a more abundant secretion of bile
and the production of icterus, we would explain by the
resorption of bile fron the surface of the intestine. In
other circumstances, the icterus results manifestly from
an alteration of the blood. Thus it is that certain
animal poisons and certain miasms may be the cause
of this affection. In such cases we get most light from
the theories of Frerichs and of Kuhn, which find the
cause of the jaundice in primary alterations of the
blood.

Among the animal poisons which may provoke icterus,
we may mention, besides the virus of venomous serpents, the

special microbes of pyæmia resulting from traumatism, the puerperal state, or external causes.

The mineral poisons may also give rise to jaundice. Jaundice is often seen in acute poisoning from phosphorus, sometimes in poisoning from mercury, copper and antimony. Chloroform and ether sometimes produce jaundice.

Jaundice is often seen in different fevers; yellow fever of the tropics, marsh fevers of India and Algiers, typhoid fever, relapsing fever (observed chiefly in London, in Scotland, and in Ireland), bilious typhoid fever (Griesinger). Epidemics of icterus, of undoubted malarial origin are on record; and Quin-quaud relates the history of an epidemic of forty-six cases of benign icterus observed in 1869 in the service of Lorain.

As for those cases of icterus called *nervous icterus,* which are occasioned by strong emotions, anger, fright, etc., and which we cannot explain either by spasm or paralysis of the bile ducts, we are obliged to hypothecate disturbances of the cerebro-spinal axis and particularly of the bulbus, which determine direct modifications in the circulation of the bile in the hepatic cells—it would seem that the bile, instead of passing from the hepatic cell into the bile ducts, finds its way into the capillary net-work.

According to Frerichs, in icterus from mental emotions the troubles of innervation may conduce in two ways to the accumulation of bile in the blood:

1. By modifications in the hepatic circulation, due to the influence which the nerves exercise on the calibre of the branches of the vena portæ.

2. By perturbations in the action of the heart or in the respiratory movements, as well as in the renal secretion.

What are the therapeutic indications for the treatment of jaundice without obstruction, based on the data which I have just given? We can really effect little. In combating these kinds of jaundice, we can only attack the primary cause which has occasioned the jaundice. Oppose the alteration of the blood in cases of hæmatogenous icterus, re-establish the functions of the liver in those which are due to excess·of the biliary secretion, calm nervous perturbations in jaundice resulting from strong emotion—snch are the principal indications to fulfil in the treatment of jaundice without obstruction.

It only remains for me to speak of the third variety of icterus, namely, grave icterus. I shall endeavor to do this as briefly as possible.

Grave icterus (acute, pernicious, typhoid, hemorrhagic, essential, fatal icterus), which Monneret defines : ''a bilious, icteric, remittent, hemorrhagic and adynamic fever whose almost constant termination is death," may be observed at all ages, but it presents its maximum of frequency between the ages of 18 and 30 years. Pregnancy seems to be a predisposing cause (Charcot, Frerichs, Laborde and others). Out of 31 cases, Frerichs found 9 in the male and 22 in the female; one-half of the latter were connected with pregnancy. Lebert's statistics give 40 men and only 20 women. Syphilis is said to be a predisposing cause, also excessive labor, malaria, drunkenness, etc. The disease has prevailed epidemically within narrow areas (barracks, prisons, ships).

Grave icterus may be grave from the onset; oftener pernicious symptoms set in during the course of an attack of jaundice. In the great majority of cases softening or destruction of the liver has been found in connection with it (acute yellow atrophy.

The onset is often insidious. If sometimes the disease begins suddenly by a chill, headache, vomiting, generally the first symptom is a simple digestive disorder. The patient complains of fatigue, is in bad trim, without appetite, with a little headache, fulness at the epigastrium or over the liver. These symptoms go on increasing, the patient gets weaker and weaker. The jaundice first appears limited to the conjunctivæ, and extends to the rest of the body. Coincidently there are often hemorrhages of variable magnitude, from the bloody oozing of the gums, sanguinolent expectoration, cutaneous extravasations, to copious bleeding from stomach, nose and intestines.

The fever, which was nil or intermittent at first, becomes ordinarily remittent about the eighth day, with nocturnal exacerbation and agitation.

The debility augments, and yet there is sometimes on the part of the patient a gaiety and an indifference which contrasts singularly with the gravity of the general condition.

The intelligence remains intact; it is not till the last stages of the disease that the patient is delirious or is convulsed in the trunk and limbs; a persistent hiccough sometimes complicates the suffering of the patient.

The heart sometimes presents a murmur, due, according to Potain, to a temporary tricuspid insufficiency.

The urine shows nothing characteristic at the outset, but soon becomes of high color and may be bloody, either from passage of the coloring matter of the blood or blood itself into the renal secretion. The urea seems to augment at first, then diminishes, and may fall as low as 50 c. g. in the twenty-four hours.

Leucin, tyrosin, xanthin and hypoxanthin, sometimes albumin, are found in the urine. The microscope reveals casts and blood globules.

In cases that terminate favorably, amelioration is ushered in by a copious diuresis.

The progress of grave icterus is rapid: death sometimes supervenes the fifth or sixth day, generally from the seventh to the twelfth day. The patients succumb in a state of somnolence, coma, algidity, or in convulsions.

Although the termination is generally fatal, yet quite a number of cases of recovery have been reported.

From the above description you see that occasionally in jaundice symptoms of the greatest gravity appear. Hemorrhages from the mucous membranes supervene; cerebral disorders manifest themselves; the patient falls into profound adynamia and succumbs more or less rapidly. To explain these accidents, some have referred to the post mortem alterations noticed in patients that have succumbed to grave icterus. This is the anatomo-pathological theory maintained by Rokitansky. Others as Monneret, Ozanam, Genouville, basing themselves on the fact that the anatomo-pathological lesions may be wanting in certain cases of grave icterus, have held that the affection is a general disease of typhic nature, and that the hepatic lesions are secondary. Lastly, there is an intermediate theory which has had for supporters, Bright, Budd, Trousseau, and Vulpian, which considers malignant jaundice as the product of a general blood poisoning which smites indeed the whole economy, but more particularly the hepatic functions. Does experimental physiology throw any light on the one or the other of these theories?

Researches made in this direction have shown us, first, that bile as such, passing into the blood, never produces the symptoms of grave icterus, and that, in a word, the choletoxæmia which Lebert had invoked as the point of departure of all the symptoms supervening in malignant icterus, has not been demonstrated experimentally. Flint has incriminated but one element of the bile as the cause of the toxæmia, viz: cholesterine, and to the *choletoxæmia* of Lebert, he opposes his *cholesteræmia* as the chief factor in the toxic accidents observed. Here, also, experimentation has given a negative answer, for when you inject cholesterine into the blood you do not determine any very deleterious effect.

Moreover, destruction of the liver, which has been hypothecated as the cause of grave icterus, because favoring the accumulation or the passage of bile or of certain of its elements into the blood, cannot be accepted as the true cause, if we may rely on experimentation.

Decaudin * has alleged another cause, and has referred us to the resemblance between the symptoms of grave icterus and those of uræmia, showing that suppression of the functions of the kidney may be a consequence of the passage of the coloring matter of the bile through those emunctories.

While recognizing the importance of Decaudin's facts, it must be admitted that they do not apply to all cases of grave icterus. Perhaps we should, also, in

---

* Decaudin, Concomitance of Diseases of the Liver and Kidneys, and in particular of the Kidneys in Jaundice. (These de Paris, 1878.)

He has shown that in grave icterus the kidney is often affected with pigmentary infiltration and fatty degeneration.

He recommends us to examine the urine minutely, and to look for albumen and tube casts; he recommends also to take note of the quantity of the urea, and the presence of leucin and of tyrosin. In grave icterus the appearance of polyuria, and the augmentation of the figure of urea indicate an approaching recovery.

In certain cases of icterus the liver may be little affected, and the kidney gravely diseased. Decaudin calls this grave icterus with renal form.

explaining the grave symptoms of this kind of jaundice, give due weight to the passage into the blood of
the alkaloids of putrefaction which are incessantly absorbed from the surface of the intestine, and which it
is one of the functions of the liver to destroy, in part;
when the parenchyma of this gland is destroyed, it
is easy to understand that there may result from the
retention of these unchanged alkaloids in the system,
symptoms of the greatest gravity. This is an hypo-
thesis which applies to a great number of cases, but it
is not supported by sufficiently solid scientific proofs
to warrant us in adopting it in its application to all
cases.

We must confess, then, that the primary cause of
the toxic phenomena is wanting, and that in individuals affected with icterus there supervene, under
the influence of a special poisoning which generally,
but not constantly, produces grave lesions on the part
of the liver, pernicious symptoms such as are characteristic of the icterus which we have just been
studying.

This uncertainty in the pathogeny of grave icterus
entails an equally profound uncertainty in the treatment. Ignorant of the primary cause of this icterus,
we are ignorant of the proper therapeutic means to
combat these affections, and we can only direct our
treatment to certain of the symptoms of this grave
malady. One of the most manifest is the adynamia,
hence the necessity of a supporting treatment is insist-

ed upon by all authorities. You will then employ Peruvian bark and even quinine, by reason of the intimate relations which connect these grave hepatic troubles with certain affections of malarial nature. Give also alcoholic and other stimulants, and endeavor to combat the hemorrhages which are so prone to appear from the nasal, pulmonary and gastric mucous membranes.

There is yet another form of grave icterus which you will have to treat. I refer to that icterus which succeeds poisoning by phosphorus; this form, in fact, is peculiar in that it has a chronic course, almost without fever. You ought to prevent such untoward results by treating the symptoms of poisoning when they occur by such remedies as preparations of turpentine, but when the icterus is once declared, you have still the progressive enfeeblement of the patient as the capital symptom, and it is to this that you should address all your therapeutic efforts.

As you see, our ignorance is great respecting the special treatment of the forms of grave icterus; it is to be hoped that coincidently with future progress in experimental physiology and clinical medicine, we shall attain to a better knowledge of these affections and thereby of their treatment.

Thus far I have spoken to you in this lecture of only three kinds of icterus. It remains to me in conclusion to allude to two kinds of false jaundice, the jaundice of the newly born, and hæmaphæic jaundice.

The first of these affections has been well studied of late years by Porak* who has shown us that we are to distinguish two species of jaundice in infancy, the jaundice *of* the newly born† and jaundice *in* the newly born. The first is a simple hæmaphæic icterus, while icterus *in* the newly born is always biliphæic, *i. e.* a true icterus. As for hæmaphæic icterus, I need not remind you of the important researches which Gubler

---

*Considerations on the Icterus of the Newly Born. These de Paris, 1878.

†The icterus of the newly-born is a very frequent affection, it is observed, according to Porak, in eighty per cent. of births.

It is almost always a hæmaphæic icterus; sometimes, however, it seems to have a biliary origin, hence the distinction between the icterus of the newly-born and icterus *in* the newly born. The icterus of the newly-born is, as before said, almost always hæmaphæic, and presents itself as a benign affection of short duration.

The icterus of the newly-born may however be *biliphæic*, and then it is due to congenital lesions of the biliary passages; it is always grave. As for icterus in the newly-born, it is always symptomatic of an affection of the liver, *i. e.*, it is a true icterus. (Porak, on Icterus of the Newly-born, Paris, 1878.)

Gubler was the first to describe hæmiphæic icterus (1858) in connection wiih the icterus of lead-poisoning. This is his theory of hæmaphæic icterus: There is a great likeness between bile pigment and the coloring matter of the blood. The transformation of hæmoglobin into bile pigment takes place in the blood, and this pigment is then eliminated by the

9 x

has made on this subject; but if this affection has
given rise to labors fraught with interest from a clinical
and pathogenic point of view, it must be admitted
that as therapeutists we are still as much in the dark
as before. Therefore I can only mention these forms
and pass on to the study of engorgements of the liver,
to which I propose to devote the following lectures.

---

bile; but let the functions ot the liver be suppressed, or let
there be an excessive breaking up of the blood globules, the
hæmaphæin accumulates in the blood and produces a yellow
coloration of the integuments. We find, then, this icterus in
diseases which have a double origin; exaggerated deglobuliza-
tion (hæmaphæism of bilious fevers, hæmaturia of warm countries, icterus from certain poisons), and functional alterations
of the liver—hepatic congestion, nervous perturbations of the
liver, etc. (Gubler, Hæmaphæic Icterus in Lead-poisoning,
1857; also Article Albuminuria in Diction. Encylop, etc.)

CHAPTER V.

TREATMENT OF ENGORGEMENTS OF THE LIVER.

SUMMARY.—Engorgements of the Liver—Division of Engorgements--Degenerations of the Liver–Amyloid Degeneration, its Treatment—Fatty Degeneration, its Treatment—Cancerous Degeneration, its Treatment—Engorgements by Circulatory Troubles—Congestion of the Liver—Causes of Hepatic Congestion—Active and Passive Congestion—Treatment of Congestion of the Liver.

In taking up the treatment of engorgements of the liver I do not under-estimate the difficulties of such a task, difficulties which result especially from the multiplicity of conditions connoted by this term engorgement. This word, in fact, comprehends a great number of dissimilar affections which have only one point in common, that they are all accompanied by augmentation in the size of the liver.

I might have taken up in their proper order the various diseases of the hepatic gland, and stated in connection with each one the kind of treatment appropriate. But it has seemed to me preferable, from the point of view of the general considerations into which I desire to enter, to retain that old word—now gone out of fashion—*engorgement of the liver*, but which still possesses a real clinical value; hence I shall endeavor to pursue this difficult study with as much method as possible.

We may in a general manner group the engorgements of the liver in five special classes. In the first we may place the true degenerations of the liver, and in this group we shall study the amyloid, fatty, and cancerous degenerations of this gland.

To the second division we may assign that augmentation of volume which results from disturbances in the circulation of the organ, and hepatic congestion is the type of this group. In the third group we have enlargements produced. not by troubles in the circulation, but in the biliary excretion; *hypertrophic cirrhosis with icterus*, enters into this group. Inflammation of the liver, acute or chronic, accompanied or not with abscess, constitutes the fourth group; we shall here study the hepatites, and in particular, chronic interstitial hepatitis, described under the name of cirrhosis. Lastly, the fifth class comprehends the augmentation of volume of the liver produced by cysts, and I shall devote an entire lecture to the treatment of hydatid cysts of the liver.

You will see, gentlemen, that if the progress of clinical medicine and of pathological anatomy has greatly extended our knowledge of hepatic engorgements, therapeutics, unfortunately, has lagged behind, and there will be numerous instances in which I shall have occasion to point out the little advance which has been made in the knowledge of how to treat these diseases of the liver.

Let us take up the first group which includes the degenerations of the liver, amyloid, fatty, and cancerous. Without entering here into anatomo-pathological details which are quite outside of my subject, I shall mention the symptoms which will enable you to recognize these different alterations.

Amyloid or waxy degeneration of the liver determines the greatest engorgement of the organ; the liver becomes enormous, and sometimes fills the whole abdominal cavity. This augmentation affects uniformly the whole hepatic gland; you detect no nodules, and the liver whose lower border you can often feel through the abdominal walls, presents a hardness and a consistency like leather. This enormous engorgement of the liver is never accompanied with pain, with ascites, or with icterus, and this is a sign of the utmost importance.*

You will find this waxy degeneration chiefly in prolonged suppurations; sometimes syphilis or intermittent fever may be the starting point, but it is especially to suppurations of long standing, both in the case of the liver and of the kidney, that we are to

---

*Murchison has seen the liver of an adult affected with amyloid degeneration weighing 5500 grammes instead of 1500 to 1800 grammes the normal. .

attribute the chief influence in the production of amyloid degenerations.*

What is the treatment of amyloid degeneration of the liver ? Unhappily, we can do but little. We have, first of all, the prophylactic means which oppose amyloid degeneration, that is to say, in individuals affected with prolonged suppurations, with white swell-

---

*Hepatic syphilis presents itself under two aspects, that of interstitial hepatitis or infiltrated syphilis, and that of gummatous hepatitis or nodular syphilis. The first is characterized by special cicatricial-like depressions which modify the form of the organ. Fatty or amyloid degeneration is often also noticed. In the second species, the liver presents numerous gummata, varying in aspect, according to the period of their evolution.

As for the symptomatology of hepatic syphilis, it is very obscure. Cornil and Ranvier teach that interstitial hepatitis belongs to the second period, while the gummy form belongs to the tertiary period of syphilis.

Jaundice may appear in the course of syphilis, and may depend on acute gastric catarrh. Lacombe has noticed a case of grave syphilitic icterus.

Hepatic syphilis, mentioned in old medical works, was first described by Dietrich in 1849; it was afterwards treated of by Gubler (1852), Quelet (1856), Lecontour (1858), Virchow (1858), and still later by Leudet, Frerichs and Lancereaux, all of whom have made a complete study of the subject. (Virchow, Treatise on Tumors; Frerichs, Diseases of the Liver; Lancereaux, Historical and Practical Treatise on Syphilis; Cornil and Ranvier, Pathological Histology; Gubler, Gaz. Médicale, 1852; Lacombe, A Study on the Hepatic Accidents of Syphilis in the Adult, Thèse de Paris, 1874.)

ing, for instance, the physician should interfere early to remedy these suppurations. From the point of view of amyloid degeneration of organs, conservative surgery, in endeavoring to save limbs in spite of the grave disorders with which they may be affected, is attended with a certain danger, and it is to this fact that the advocates of resections of the joints have appealed in justification of early surgical intervention.

As special medicaments for amyloid degeneration, I shall mention only iodine and the iodides, on the one hand, and the ammoniacal salts on the other.

Murchison vaunts the tincture of iodine of the B. Ph., which he gives in the dose of ten to fifteen drops. You can also use iodide of potassium in the dose of 15 to 30 grains.*

We are indebted to the English physicians for the principal clinical data respecting the ammoniacal salts in the treatment of hepatic affections, and particularly

---

*Murichison says that he has sometimes witnessed amelioration after the prolonged employment of nitric acid associated with certain vegetable bitters (gentian or quinine).

He also speaks well of the external usage of nitro-muriatic acid; two fluidounces of nitro-muriatic acid to nine litres of water, heated to 35° or 36° C.

The feet are immersed in this bath, the legs and thighs are sponged with it, and it is freely applied over the region of the liver, while the abdomen is swathed with a flannel cloth wrung out of this solution.

This bath should be continued half an hour, and be repeated morning and evening.

of amyloid degeneration. You may employ the chloride or carbonate of ammonium, but it is especially the ammonium chloride which is recommended, and this salt it to be given in the dose of from five to ten grains three times a day. Budd and Washburton Begbie have vaunted the effects of this medicine. But as you may imagine, these are remedies which are very uncertain, and which oftener have no well-marked results on the amyloid degeneration.*

Steatosis of the liver determines a less increase of size than amyloid degeneration; the gland is less hard, and, as is the case with amyloid liver, there is never any pain, icterus, or ascites.

You will meet with fatty degeneration under these conditions: sometimes in individuals with polysarcia, in whom you have not only fatty liver, but also fatty heart and fatty kidneys; sometimes in phthisis, and in

---

*Ammonium chloride (sal ammoniac, muriate of ammonia, hydrochlorate of ammonia) is a salt in common use, of disagreeable taste, whose pungency may be partly overcome by combining it with extract of licorice. Thus by rubbing up equal parts of the extract of licorice and ammonium chloride, you have a preparation which can without difficulty be taken by the patient in doses of a scruple in water *ter die*. Has been recommended in bronchitis (acute or chronic), in catarrhal affections generally, in acute rheumatism (Dujardin-Beaumetz). According to Murchison, sal ammoniac in scruple doses *bis vel ter die* causes diaphoresis, augments the urinary secretion, diminishes congestions of the portal system, and relieves pains which have their seat in the liver.—TR.

fact it is oftenest met with in this disease, and we may truly say that in the autopsies of tuberculous patients fatty degeneration is the rule. Lastly, in deaths from chronic alcoholism you find this degeneration, and I recall to your mind the autopsy of a patient where many of you were present; this man ended his career of drunkenness by imbibing a quantity of brandy in the lees, and the liver presented a fine specimen of fatty disease.*

As fatty degeneration of the liver is not accompanied by any very characteristic symptoms, and plays but a secondary part in the diseases which I have just mentioned so that the attention of the physician is rarely called to this engorgement, it results that but little has been done for the therapeutics of this affection.

What we know, is that we ought, as far as possible,

---

* Besides alcoholism and pulmonary tuberculosis, other diseases may be accompanied with fatty engorgement of the liver; such are cancer and ulceration of the stomach, chronic dysentery and consumptive affections. An inappropriate diet, or diet rich with fatty matters, over-eating, life in a warm, damp and marshy climate, may bring about this steatosis. Frerichs' tables, which give the results of a multitude of post-mortem and microscopical examinations of persons who had died at the hospital Allerheiligen, at Breslau, show that fatty liver is met with at its maximum in pulmonary tuberculosis, then in pyæmia, then in cirrhosis of the liver, and, lastly, now and then in certain diseases, as pleurisy, Bright's disease, and typhus.

by a proper hygienic treatment, to get rid of the fat which tends to accumulate in the various tissues; gymnastics, rhythmical movements and daily exercise are then to be counselled. We ought also to endeavor to promote respiration, in order to consume these fatty matters, and we should prevent their introduction into the economy by the food. This fact has a certain importance when, in phthisical patients for instance, you have detected fatty degeneration of the liver; here you should prohibit cod-liver oil. As medicines, we can do no better than prescribe alkalies under all their forms, and particularly the sodic bicarbonate waters Vichy, Vals, etc.

I shall be brief, and for good practical reasons, concerning cancer of the liver. At the same time, as this affection may be confounded with other hepatic engorgements, you will have occasion to treat it; and in this connection I recall to mind a patient who was sent to me by my pupil and confrère Dr. Doumanges, of Forges.

This ·patient was suffering from chronic icterus, which had brought about such a cachectic state that one could almost affirm the existence of cancer from his very appearance; nevertheless it was nothing of the kind, for he got well under the influence of a treatment long continued, consisting in the employment of calomel, of milk diet, and of alkalies.

Ordinarily in cancer of the liver you find this organ very much increased in size, and stuffed with cancerous nodules which give it a characteristic form. These nodules are of variable size and consistency according as they have undergone development and regression; some are hard and resistant, others are of soft and almost liquid character.

Several varieties of cancer have been found in the liver; scirrhus, which is by no means rare, the encephaloid which is much the most common, and which may be accompanied by a considerable development of the blood-vessels (carcinoma hæmatodes). Lastly, in exceptional cases, you observe melanotic cancers.

To explain the frequency of cancer of the liver as a secondary affection, authorities have assumed the passage of cancerous elements by the portal vein from the diseased organ to the liver. It very frequently occurs in connection with cancer of the stomach. According to Murchison, women are oftener the subjects of hepatic cancer than men.

What then are the characters which enable you to distinguish cancerous from other degenerations of the liver? In cancerous degeneration there is certainly augmentation of volume of the organ, but this augmentation does not affect the whole gland, it occurs only in places, and for this very reason markedly alters the normal form of the gland. In certain cases you can feel through the abdominal walls the hard nodosities or lumps, as large as a chestnut or larger; these are characteristic of cancer. There is in all cases more or less pain, sometimes intense and persistent icterus, and in half the cases there is ascites.*

Add, moreover, that from a clinical point of view,

*The liver may take on a great increase of size in a very short time. Budd cites a case in which the liver, having become cancerous, weighed seven times the ordinary weight. He has also seen a cancerous mass weighing five pounds form in the course of five months; while Farre reports the case of

cancer of the liver in the majority of cases is secondary to cancer elsewhere; out of 91 cases Frerichs
found but 22 in which the liver was primarily affected,
and 35 were consecutive to cancer of the stomach.
It results from this that you will almost always observe
in patients affected with cancer of this organ, disorders
indicating a degeneration of the same nature in another part of the abdominal cavity. Here you will
employ for treatment hypodermics of morphine to
allay the pain; you will prescribe milk diet; you will
combat the icterus by the appropriate means already
mentioned; you will support the forces of the patient.
You must be persevering in your treatment, and notwithstanding the certainty of your diagnosis, you can
always hope that possibly you have made a mistake,
and that you may yet triumph over the disease which
you have before you.

I now proceed to take up a disease of the liver
which is extremely frequent, and on which therapeutics has a real influence; I refer to the engorgement
determined by the troubles in the circulation of the
liver.

---

an hepatic cancer which increased in weight by five pounds in
ten days.

The pain in cancer of the liver is more or less acute, especially on pressure over the organ. It radiates into the
shoulders, the back and the loins; it is sometimes paroxysmal,
and lancinating; is rarely absent, especially in cases that grow
rapidly. (Budd, Diseases of the Liver, 1855; Farre, Morbid
Anatomy of the Liver, 1812).

Whenever, from any cause, the blood accumulates in the liver, this accumulation produces an increase in the size of the organ. Monneret, who has made a careful study of hepatic congestion, has shown that the liver, which in the normal state weighs about 1,600 grams may acquire, when forcibly injected with blood, a weight of more than 2,500 grams. This augmentation of weight manifests itself by an augmentation of volume, and one of the first symptoms of congestive engorgement is the marked increase of size of organ. These congestions present themselves under two aspects : sometimes they are active, sometimes passive. Let us see under what circumstances they are produced.

The congestion is passive, when, for instance, it is linked to a cardio-pulmonary trouble. Recall to mind what I told you while speaking of the treatment of mitral lesions, and you will remember that always, at an advanced period of their course, these affections are accompanied by a passive and chronic congestion of the liver.* I have dwelt at some length on these congestions and their treatment, and I have endeavored to make clear the difference which exists between cardiac cirrhosis and true cirrhosis. The circulatory disorders of the lungs, tumors of the mediastinum, and, in general, all causes which hinder the emptying of the inferior vena cava, have the same result.

---

* See Diseases of the Heart, Vol. I, page 131 (G. S. Davis' Library Ed.).

As for active congestions, they are due to a variety of causes; in a great number of cases their origin is gastro-intestinal. You readily understand the influence of diet on congestions of this gland, as the liver receives from the portal vein all the liquid substances introduced into the digestive tube; so when the food is of too exciting a nature, and, especially, when too prolonged usage has been made of alcoholic drinks, such intemperance entails as a certain conse-quence a congestion of this organ; the inflammations of the digestive tube have the same effect, and are propagated to the liver; hence we see hepatic stases accompany or follow any phlegmasia of the stomach or intestines.

There is another affection of the digestive tube which is always attended with congestion of the liver; I refer to dilatation of the stomach. Bouchard was the first to call our attention to this point, and it is proba-able that this congestion is caused by the passage into the liver of toxic substances occasioned by impairment of the gastric digestion.

Sometimes also the hyperæmia is linked to a gen-eral diathetic state, and you will see in arthritic patients congestion of the liver more or less severe. Gout and even rheumatism may have the same effect, and you know that clinical medicine has recognized a particular form of icterus having such origin: rheu-matic icterus.

Lastly, in certain circumstances, hyperæmia of the

liver takes the place of the physiological congestion of certain organs ; and when in females there occurs an abrupt suppression of the menses, or in men the sudden cessation of a hemorrhoidal flux, there sometimes supervenes in these cases a hepatic congestion which is vicarious or supplementary.

This rapid pathogenetic description of congestion of the liver would be incomplete if I did not point out in connection therewith the influence of the atmosphere on hepatic stasis. It is, in fact, in certain zones, and under the influence of certain climates that these hyperæmias of the liver are almost sure to occur, and it may be affirmed that there is hardly a European living in the torrid zone who has not suffered more or less from congestions of this organ.

Malaria very often adds its influence to that of climate in modifying the hepatic functions, and in marshy countries you will notice at some stage more or less advanced of intermittent fever, a congestion of the hepatic gland.

These hyperæmias of the liver are either acute or chronic. In our climate, and apart from traumatism, we see but little of the acute congestions of the liver; it is generally the chronic forms that we have to treat. Whether they be active or passive,* the congestions of

---

*Baillon, **Portal and Andral have observed congestion of the liver in** scurvy. Hyperæmia **of the liver has also been noticed in** poisoning by lead, **by phosphorous and by curare.**

the liver manifest themselves by the following train of symptoms:

There is first of all an increase in the size of the liver, an augmentation which affects the whole organ; then there is pain, which is never wanting. This pain is seated in the hepatic region; it often encircles the base of the thorax like a girdle, and radiates into neighboring parts and particularly the shoulder of the right side; almost always there is a slight jaundice, characterized by a sub-icteric tent of the conjunctivæ and skin.

Monneret, who has carefully studied hyperæmia of the liver and its causes, gives the following etiological division:

A. *Hyperæmia by disease of the organs:* 1, Diseases of the circulatory organs (according to Monneret, the hepatic circulation is the *first partial circulation* disturbed in diseases of the heart); 2, Cancerous and tuberculous diseases of the liver.

B. Hyperæmia by alteration of the blood: 1, by plethora (Monneret affirms that these sorts of hepatic congestions are disputable); 2, by dissolution of the blood (typhus, yellow fever, diphtheria, puerperal fever); 3, by diminution of albumen; 4, by presence of pus in the blood; 5, by virulent diseases (syphilis, glanders); 6, by diathetic diseases (scrofula and rheumatism); 7, by malarial poisoning.

C. Dynamic hyperæmia: 1, by secretory hyperæmia (Monneret includes in this group the congestion which accompanies icterus called essential or spasmodic); 2, hyperæmia vicarious of another flux (suppression of menses and of hemorrhoids); 3, physiological hyperæmia (Monneret includes in this group the congestion which follows the digestion of certain aliments (Monneret, Pathologie Interne, 1861–1863).

These congestions are accompanied by a fever, which Monneret has well studied, a fever with paroxysms which come on between four and five o'clock in the afternoon. Lastly, patients affected with intense congestion of the liver complain of respiratory difficulty, a veritable dyspnœa, which is to be referred to the cardiac troubles consecutive to the hepatic affections of which we have just spoken. Such are, in brief, the principal symptoms determined by hyperæmia of the liver.

The treatment varies according to the cause which has determined the afflux of blood; and that of active hyperæmia of the liver is widely different from the treatment which is suited to the congestion determined by mechanical troubles in the cardio-pulmonary circulation. This latter congestion, you know, depends generally on a mitral affection, and already under diseases of the heart I have set forth the treatment proper for these passive congestions.* Our remedies, in fact, are not directed primarily to the liver, but to the heart, and you have at this moment in one of our wards a good example of these hepatic and cardiac congestions. I refer to a patient whom I have before pointed out to you in Ward St. Lazare, who is suffering from mitral lesions with enormous congestion of the liver, and in whom, by the use of digitalis alone, we

---

* See Diseases of the Heart, vol. I, (Library Ed. G. S. Davis.)

10 X

have succeeded in diminishing by one half, the volume of the hepatic gland.

As for chronic or subacute hyperæmia·originating under the influence of a general diathesis or of modifications effected in the gastro-intestinal tube, you can place most reliance on the following means:

1st. The revulsive method: large fly blisters have a marked resolvent action on hyperæmia of the liver, and I have always derived from them excellent results. Monneret places great importance on the revulsive method, and I have been surprised not to see mention made of this powerful curative agent in the excellent article of Murchison on the treatment of hepatic congestion.

Local blood lettings have also been advised for congestions of the liver, especially for those which have an acute course and a phlegmasic character; you apply over the hepatic region where the pain is most severe, from six to ten wet cups or a dozen leeches; you may also apply the leeches, not over the liver, but to the anus; this practice, which has been much vaunted by my colleague Rendu, causes disappearance of the hepatic pains. But I advise you to reserve this spoliative method for plethoric persons and those in whom the hepatic congestion manifests itself by very intense symptoms, for in general I am not a strenuous advocate of blood lettings in diseases of the liver; these withdrawals of blood almost always entail perturbations which manifest themselves by hemorrhages, so frequently observed in hepatic affections.

You should always employ internally medicaments which act as cholagogues, and it is in these cases that calomel gives marvellous results; thus in arthritic patients, for example, who have a tendency to hepatic congestion, you will see the symptoms determined by this hyperæmia rapidly disappear under the usage of calomel in small doses, two grains a day, for instance. You can add to this treatment enonymin and the other cholagogues; chloride of ammonium has also been employed, especially in India, in the treatment of hepatic congestion. Lastly, do not forget that cold lavements, which I have already recommended in the treatment of catarrhal jaundice, may here appropriately find their place.

It is also in these congestions that a certain remedy is said to do good which has a great reputation in South America, and especially in Chili, namely boldo.

I have studied this medicament with Claude Verne, and have shown that the tincture of boldo, and especially the essence, has an action not only on the liver but also on the kidneys, and it is probably by the enhanced diuresis that it acts indirectly on the hepatic diseases.*

---

*In Chili boldo is considered as having stomachic, carminative, and diaphoretic properties. Claude Gay affirms that it is a popular remedy for diseases of the liver.

Boldo (Peumus boldus) is a tree which grows chiefly in Chili. The leaves are the medicinal part. Analyzed, they give

But of all the curative means employed in chronic hyperæmia of the liver, the most effective, certainly, is the thermal treatment. Here we witness the triumph of Vichy and of Carlsbad; it is probable that Vichy bears the palm over its rival, and one can truly say that there is hardly a patient in this country affected with chronic hepatic congestion who has not been to these spas for relief.

By the side of these waters we should also place a heroic remedy, hydrotherapy. In the active congestions determined generally by alimentary excesses

---

an essential oil, a bitter principle boldine, citric acid, lime, sugar, gum, and tannin. The most important product of the plant is the essence which is contained in great quantity in the leaves. The bitter principle boldine has, according to Bourgoin and Verne, all the characters of an alkaloid. Different preparations are made with boldo; there is a tincture, made by macerating one part of the bruised leaves with five parts of alcohol at 60°. The wine is made thus: macerate for twenty-four hours one part of the bruised leaves with two parts of alcohol and add 3⅓ parts of Madeira wine; macerate eight days, express and filter. There is also a syrup and an elixir; the latter is made by displacing 200 grammes of bruised leaves with alcohol at 60°. In some experiments made on man and animals, Dujardin-Beaumetz has shown that the essence of boldo, in passing out by the kidneys, provokes an abundant diuresis, and that the urine has a marked odor of essence of boldo. In man, the tincture of boldo produces a sense of heat and of general stimulation. These experiments show that boldo ought to be classed among the excitant medicaments. By its tincture boldo belongs to the class of aromatic plants,

or by malarial poisoning, Fleury has shown the benefit which may be derived from the employment of the cold douche.

How ought this douche to be administered? Permit me here to interpose a word of caution. It is not enough that you should simply prescribe hydrotherapy, you should also indicate the temperature of the water, the duration of the douche and the manner of administering it.

The ignorance, unfortunately too prevalent, concerning the rules for the practice of hydrotherapy, often results in the attending physician finding his directions misunderstood, either by the physician in charge of the thermal establishment, or by the assistant to whom is intrusted the care of giving the douche.

How then will you order the administration of hydrotherapy in these cases? You will see that a

---

and like the latter it is a general diffusible stimulant and a promoter of the digestive functions; by its essence it resembles the gums and resins, and like these, it has a stimulating action on the urinary functions. Dujardin-Beaumetz has employed the tincture and the wine in cases of anæmia and dyspepsia; he gives one to two grams of the tincture (15 to 30 drops), and sixty grams (two ounces) of the wine per day. He has administered the essence of boldo in capsules in the dose of five or six grains a day in cases of catarrh of the bladder, whether acute or chronic. This dose should be given at meal time. (Bourgoin and Verne on Boldo, Jour. de Pharmacie, May, 1872; Dujardin-Beaumetz and Claude Verne, A Study of Boldo, Bull. de Therap., t. lxxxiv, p. 165.)

cold jet douche is given over the liver; in order that the action may be more local, you will place the sub-ject in such a manner that with the right arm slightly raised, the thigh of the same side half bent, he may receive over the hepatic region, the jet of cold water. The duration of the douche should be very short. I can not too much insist on this point. I sometimes see practitioners order douches of from four to five minutes duration; this is a great mistake. In the great majority of cases, the douche should not exceed thirty seconds duratlon, and generally fifteen seconds suffice.

Beni Barde counsels in these cases of congestion of the liver the Scotch or alternating douche *i. e.*, the douche in which, in the space of a minute, the cold douche and the warm douche are given alternately.

Lastly, when the patient manifests too great ner-vous irritability, when, instead of ameliorating the state of the liver, these douches augment the volume of the organ, you may begin by the employment of the swan's neck douche. This name is given to a douche administered with an instrument which resembles the swan's neck, and which projects along the vertebral column a considerable volume of water, but at low pressure.

Next to thermal medication and hydrotherapy, but almost on the same level as a therapeutic agency, comes the dietetic treatment. As in a great number of cases, the active congestions of the liver have for their cause a too abundant and too stimulating diet, you readily understand that milk, which gives such good results in the treatment of the other hepatic affections, is also particularly indicated in the treatment of hepatic hyperæmias. You ought then, not only to regulate minutely the alimentary regimen of patients, but to prohibit all substances which may bring about a congestion of the liver.

But before ordering a milk diet, you must ascertain whether there exists or not any dilatation of the stomach; in cases where the stomach is dilated, you should prohibit an exclusive milk diet, and subject the patient to the alimentary regimen proper to gastroectasis. It is because different authorities have not sufficiently made account of this distinction, that milk diet in the treatment of congestion of the liver has been considered by some as favorable, by others as injurious.

Such are the principal therapeutic indications to be fulfilled in the treatment of hepatic congestions. These indications will be complete if you add to them such as spring from the *indicatio causalis*, but this implies a treatment which is variable and into the study of which I cannot enter, but must refer you to what I have said respecting the etiology of hepatic congestions, and I pass now to another group of hepatic engorgements.

At the beginning of this lecture I mentioned among the causes of engorgements of the liver, disturbances in the excretion of the bile. I now come to the study of these engorgements. In my experimental researches with Audigé on spasm of the bile ducts, I noticed that when in a dog we tied the common bile duct, we determined a considerable dilatation of all the biliary passages intra and extra hepatic, which causes a considerable increase in the size of the liver. I have, moreover, shown you, when speaking of the obstructions of the ductus choledochus, the alterations of the hepatic parenchyma therefrom resulting, and which amount to a veritable cirrhosis taking its origin in the bile ducts; but this cirrhosis of biliary origin may also come about spontaneously; it is this form which Hayem, Cornil and Harnot have described under the name of *hypertrophic cirrhosis with icterus.*

This cirrhosis, which is a true generalized angiocholitis, producing a secondary sclerosis around the distended canaliculi, presents the following symptoms: the liver is uniformly hypertrophied, there is a sharp pain on pressure over the region of the liver; lastly, jaundice always accompanies this affection, But this icterus presents this particular character that it varies in intensity from one day to another during the course of the disease. There is not, ordinarily, any ascites in this form of cirrhosis.

This affection generally resists all means of treatment, and notwithstanding the very precise notions furnished by pathological anatomy respecting the special processes of this cirrhosis, we know of no

curative treatment. Cholagogues, revulsives, and tonics
have been all tried, but tried in vain.*

It remains for me in concluding the subject of
engorgements of the liver to study such as are pro-

---

* The history of hypertrophic cirrhosis is of quite recent
date. It was Olivier, of Rouens, who, in 1871, first separated
this affection from ordinary cirrhosis, then the researches of
Hayem and Cornil, in 1875, showed the alterations of the bile
ducts, while Harnot, in 1876, gave a complete description of
this affection.

When you examine the anatomo-pathological lesions of
hypertrophic cirrhosis, you observe that it is characterized by
an alteration effecting essentially the intra and extra lobular
biliary canaliculi. These ducts are dilated and often obliterated
by an infiltration of pigmentary granules.

This idiopathic angiocholitis determines an increase in
the connective tissue frame-work, a veritable sclerosis, which
Charcot has described under the name of insular sclerosis,
which is generally circumscribed to a single lobule, and sys-
tematically invades the periphery of this lobule.

As symptoms, hypertrophic cirrhosis is always accompanied by a very considerable augmentation of the liver, with
jaundice more or less pronounced, without ascites, and without
augmentation of the collateral venous circulation.

As for the prognosis, it is most grave, and thus far all
cases have terminated by death.

Latterly, Litten has combatted the views of Charcot respecting the pathogeny of hypertrophic cirrhosis; he does not
believe, for instance, that this affection originates in stagnation
of the bile.

Repeating Charcot's experiments on the effects of ligature
of the choledochus, he notices that the lesions of insular cir-

duced by inflammation. This is an important topic which merits your special attention, and to this I shall devote my next lecture.

---

rhosis do not take place when antiseptic precautions are used; on the other hand, they are produced when you irritate power-fully, by means of croton oil, the mucous membrane of the bile passages. Litten concludes that it is not to biliary stasis, but to inflammation of the bile ducts, that the pathogeny of hyper-trophic cirrhosis should be ascribed.

Lastly, from a clinical point of view, according to Litten, the diagnosis between the two varieties of cirrhosis, true cir-rhosis and hypertrophic cirrhosis is often impossible, although intense icterus belongs only to the hypertrophic form.

According to Lancereaux, it will not do to confound hyper-trophic cirrhosis with the grave icterus which sometimes accompanies cirrhosis in the alcoholic. In these cases the bile ducts have neither undergone proliferation nor alteration, at the same time the sclerosis is insular and unilobular.(a)

(a) Olivier, Mémoire sur la cirrhose hypertroph. (Union médicale, 1874, p. 361).—Hayem, Contribution à l'étude de l'hépatite interstitielle chronique avec hypertrophie du foie (Arch. de phys., 1874, p. 126).—Cornil, Anatomie pathologique de la cirrhose (Arch. de phys., 1874, p. 365).—Hanot, Etude sur une forme de cirrhose hypertrophique du foie (Thèse de Paris, 1876).—Charcot et Gombault. Sur les altérations du foie consécutives à la ligature du canal cholédoque, 1876, p. 272 et 453.—Litten, Ueber die biliare Form der Lebercirrhose u. den diagnostichen Werth der Icteriis (Charité Annalen de 1879, p. 152. Berlin, 1880).—Pierre Dupont, De l'hépatite inter-stitielle diffuse aignë. Thèse de Paris, 1878.

CHAPTER VI.

TREATMENT OF INFLAMMATIONS OF THE LIVER.

SUMMARY.—The Inflammations of the Liver—Acute and Chronic Inflammations—Hepatitis of Warm Countries —Abscess of the Liver—Pathogeny—Therapeutic Indications — Aspiration — Opening of the Abscess—Slow Processes—Rapid Processes—Accidents Consecutive to the Opening of Abscesses of the Liver—Chronic Inflammation of the Liver—Interstitial Hepatitis or Cirrhosis—Its Nature—Its Frequency—Symptoms of Cirrhosis—Treatment of Cirrhosis—Paracentesis for Ascites in Cirrhosis—Indications and Contra-Indications.

GENTLEMEN.—In the last lecture I included inflammation of the liver in the group of engorgements of this organ. It is the treatment of these inflammations which I intend to set forth to-day. As I desire to confine myself within the limits indicated by the title which I have given to this course (Clinical Therapeutics), I shall occupy your time only with those affections which we meet in our wards, and with diseases of which you can watch the progress, and judge the effects of the treatment. Therefore I shall not attempt a complete study of hepatitis properly so-called, a disease which is not observed in our country, and to which has been given the name of the hepatitis of warm climates. You will find, moreover, in the remarkable works of our confreres of the marine service, and in the writings of the English physicians who, practising in the colonies, and in particular in India, have very frequent opportunities for observing this kind of hepatitis, precepts and useful data on this subject. What we find in our hospital service, under our climate, is the result of this hepatitis contracted in the tropics, a suppurative hepatitis, which produces voluminous abscesses of the liver, and at this moment, in this very hospital you can see in the wards of my colleague and friend, Perier, a fine instance of these abscesses brought on by living in a hot climate. The hepatitis of warm countries, when it is not due to traumatism or to an alteration of the digestive passages, may be determined by rapid chilling of the body while sweating, and sudden suppression of perspiration by excessive drinking of cold water, etc.

This disease, frequent in India and in the tropical countries generally, is not equally grave in the French colonies; hence it is quite rare at Cayenne, while frequent and very fatal at Martinique and Senegal.

As Dutrouleau remarks, the endemic hepatitis of hot climates passes through different stages which have their distinct characters: to the three anatomical characters, congestion, inflammation, suppuration, correspond certain symptoms which give to the disease a special physiognomy.

To the form which is the most mild, has been sometimes given the name of the dominant symptom "liver ache" (*point de coté*); the denominations acute and chronic hepatitis indicate the disease arrived at the stage of phlegmasia corresponding to these two forms; abscess of the liver indicates the disease gone on to suppuration.

The pain in the side corresponds to active hyperæmia. Sometimes suddenly, after fatigues or excesses, the patient is taken with an excruciating pain in the right side, exasperated by pressure and strong inspirations. This pain by degrees becomes less, then disappears, to return after the least fatigue or excess. Sometimes the disease is confined to this one symptom, and the patient gets well; if it continues its progress, it soon goes on to the second and third stages.

Habitually, the hepatitis begins by an accession of fever with a chill, heat, and sweats; then supervenes an excruciating, lancinating pain, which obliges the patient to writhe and draw himself up in his bed; at the same time there is a considerable difficulty of breathing, which auscultation does not sufficiently explain.

When the crisis is passed, the patient still experiences the pain, which is less intense, and which almost always corresponds to an inflamed point in the liver. Dutrouleau attaches a great importance in diagnosis to a sympathetic pain which the patient sometimes experiences in the right shoulder, and which indicates an inflammation of the convex surface of the organ.

If the patient is to get well, the pain little by little disappears, leaving only a little soreness behind. If the disease passes to the chronic stage, the pain becomes intermittent, lancinating, while the fever becomes high if the hepatitis goes on to suppuration. Jaundice does not always exist after the crisis; sometimes there is a straw-yellow color of the skin, a simple icteric pallor, with slight discoloration of the sclerotics; the urine is red and scanty, and does not contain the coloring matters of the bile, except when the icterus is intense.

When the hepatitis goes on to suppuration, the liver becomes tumefied and protuberant, and sometimes bulging is detected at the point where the abscess is seated.

Abscesses of the liver are superficial or deep, are oftener seated in the right lobe than in the left (in 122 out of 136 cases), · They differ from metastatic or pyæmic abscesses, which have a brown color, are small, situated at the surface, and do not possess a pyogenic membrane. The abscesses of hepatitis are generally single. Out of 66 Dutrouleau found 41 in which there was but one; 16 in which there were 2; 5 in which there were 3. Lastly, out of these 66 cases there were 56 large abscesses, i. e., the size of an orange at least, and 10 small ones.

The pus of recent abscesses is yellow, creamy, and inodorous; that of old abscesses is brown, the color of wine dregs, **sometimes** contains blood or the debris **of the organ; takes on** an ammoniacal, sometimes putrid odor.

When surgical interference is not resorted to, **the abscess, if not too** large, **may get** well by absorption; **else** it increases **in** size from day **to** day, and the patient, by **reason of** the progress of the disease, falls into a profound **adynamia,** and dies of exhaustion. Under other **circumstances, the pus** dissects for itself a passage externally, or **into the neighboring** organs. If there are peritoneal adhesions, **it may burrow its** way through the abdominal walls; **in** other cases **it bursts into the peritoneal cavity, and causes** a rapidly fatal **peritonitis. If the abscess opens into the** pericardium, **death does not long delay, but if it opens into** the bronchi, **the stomach, or the colon, recovery may sometimes take place.** Murchison relates **such a case of recovery in a physician whose abscess opened into the bronchi.**

But before taking up the treatment of hepatic abscesses, allow me a short digression concerning their origin. I have just told you that these purulent collections are the consequence of suppurative hepatitis; I thus touched upon an important question in their pathogeny. In fact, in the opinion of a great number of observers, abscesses of the liver do not result from hepatitis, but from dysentery; the ulcerations of the intestines determine the passage of septic matters into the portal circulation and the transference of these matters into the substance of the liver, causing abscesses more or less voluminous. I myself saw in this very city, while clinical chief under Behier, an abscess consecutive to dysentery. The fact then is settled; but must we therefrom conclude that all the hepatic abscesses of warm countries have this intestinal origin? By no means. Murchison maintains that generally these abscesses are the consequence of the inflammation, and that if dysentery exists, it is only a coincidence, a coincidence by the way which is very frequent, as dysentery and hepatic inflammation are two affections which are endemic in the tropical zone.

Whether they result from an hepatic inflammation or are due to dysentery, abscesses of the liver present themselves under the following form: they are fluctuating tumors, sometimes of enormous size, which unequally augment the volume of the gland; these tumors are generally slow, are accompanied, like every suppurating swelling, with accessions of intermittent or remittent fever; sometimes, however, the fever is wanting. These abscesses, if left to themselves, may open externally into the intestine or into the peritoneum, or they may dissect for themselves a passage through the lungs and pleura.

What treatment is advisable in such cases? We find ourselves in the presence of opinions which are diametrically opposite. Budd maintains that it is best not to interfere; Murray, Murchison, Cameron, Martin and others urge the most prompt possible surgical interference.. This latter practice is the one which you should follow, for not to render surgical aid is to greatly increase the chances of death; and this is not, gentlemen, a haphazard assertion, but one based on trustworthy statistics, which show that out of 120 cases of abscess of the liver left without operation, there is a mortality of 80 per cent., while by suitable surgical intervention this mortality is reduced to 32 per cent.*

Moreover, gentlemen, you know that all surgical operations on the liver are made at the present day with extreme facility, and with little or no danger. Thanks to the aspirators of Dieulafoi and Potain, we can now puncture the hepatic gland with safety, and if it happens for any reason that we do not hit the fluctuating sac, no harm results from the operation.

Lavigerie has made experiments on animals to judge of the innocuousness of punctures of the liver. He practised in dogs fine exploratory punctures, and killed the animals three days after, and however numerous were these trocar punctures, he never found any lesion of the hepatic parenchyma.

The Medico Chirurgical Society of Alexandria has reproduced these experiments on cattle, horses and dogs, and has obtained similar results.

If we may trust the reports of the English physicians who practise in India, and make almost daily use of the aspirator, as they are able to render assistance at the onset of the abscess, we cannot help believing that these punctures always relieve the patient,

*The Medico-Chirurgical Society of Alexandria in Egypt has given the most complete statistics concerning abscesses of the liver. Out of 123 cases of hepatic suppurations, 80 per cent. of those on whom no operation was performed died, while 32 per cent. that received surgical help got well. In cases of large abscesses, there was a mortality of 88 per cent. among those where there was no operation, to offset 68 per cent. of recoveries where surgical aid was early resorted to. (Bulletin de la Soc. Med.-chir. d'Alexandrie, 1867.)

even when they do not bring away pus, by producing a local letting of blood in the inflamed gland.

However this may be, we ought always, before resorting to a more active kind of treatment, to practise these aspiratory punctures. In the hepatic abscess of warm countries, this simple operation may suffice, but ordinarily this is not a curative method, and it is necessary to have recourse to other processes in order to give a free issue to the pus, and to wash out the sac by antiseptic syringings.

These processes, which pertain to the domain of surgery, are some of them slow, others rapid; I will give you a more complete account of them when I come to the treatment of hydatid cysts, and will only briefly allude to them here.

The slow processes are recommended principally by Graves and Recamier. Graves has advised an operation similar to that proposed by Begin in the treatment of hepatic cysts; i. e. he counsels to incise the abdominal walls down as far as the peritoneum, then to wait till nature makes the opening through that membrane. Recamier prefers the application of caustics, and the process is the same as that described for the opening of hydatid cysts. It is the process which Perier employed in the case of which I have before spoken.

Recamier places **over the spot** where the tumor points, from 3 to 5 grains of **caustic potash**; he thus obtains an eschar of 3 or 4 c. m. in **extent**. Then, **when** this is detached, he

11 X

puts in the wound a new piece of caustic potash, and repeats the operation till the abscess opens.

Graves incises the soft parts to within 3 or 4 m. m. of the abscess, fills the wound with charpie, and waits till the suppurative inflammation has brought about the opening of the sac.

Begin cuts down to the peritoneum and waits till by the progress of the inflammation the abscess bursts outwardly.

But the rapid processes are preferred to-day, and authorities seem to attach less importance than formerly to the formation of adhesions, relying on the fact that in the abscesses of hot countries the hepatitis will have determined at the very outset of the affection the adhesions which are sought for, therefore the method of Cambray seems to have prevailed, who advises to enter the sac at once and by direct incision. This is also the practice of Dutrouleau, who first makes an aspiratory puncture into the sac, then by means of the canula left in place and used as a grooved director, he incises the tissues and at one sweep makes a large opening into the abscess.

This practice has since been perfected, and with antiseptic precautions and Lister's dressings, the custom is now to open these abscesses altogether with the bistoury. This is the mode of treatment successfully employed and heralded by a physician at Shang-Haï, Louis Stromeyer Little.*

---

*Little's success under rigid antisepsis has been complete. The operation is done under the spray, with a long bistoury. To facilitate the issue of pus, a pair of dressing case forceps

With regard to a choice between the methods, this must depend upon circumstances. When you have to do with an immense abscess causing a marked bulging of the hepatic region, and by its very size producing profound disorders, you will employ the rapid process, that of Cambay, or of Dutrouleau, modified by Little. When, on the other hand, the abscess is of small size, and the operation less urgent, you may have recourse to the method of Recamier, a process which is not so long as one would think, as with repeated applications of caustics it is possible for you in two days easily to reach the liver. You can act even more promptly by resorting, not to the caustics, but to the Paquelin cautery. You will thus be renewing the practice which, from time immemorial, the negro empirics have followed in the treatment of abscesses of the liver in their countrymen.

They pass back and forth over a point of the hepatic region a red-hot iron, then at the end of several days they make a free opening with the knife.

Accorking to Bordier, the Negro operators of Senegal base their procedure on the fact which they have observed (and which is, moreover, perfectly exact), that a burn made on a point of the abdominal wall determines an adhesive inflammation of the peritoneum which corresponds to this point.*

is introduced and the blades forcibly separated; then the abscess is washed out with a $\frac{1}{80}$ carbolic solution, and a large drainage tube inserted. The whole is covered with Lister's dressing (Bull. de Therap., txcix, p. 408).

* Bordier, Treatment of Abscess of the Liver in Senegal (Jour. de Thérap., 1880).

Now that surgeons, thanks to the antiseptic treatment, boldly enter the abdominal cavity, the rapid processes are coming more and more into vogue, and have pretty generally superseded the slow methods. An abscess of the liver is considered just like a collection of pus elsewhere, to be freely opened, at whatever depth it exists.

Whether you have recourse to the slow or to the rapid processes, when once the sac is open, care must be taken to make antiseptic lavages with solutions of chloral, or of boric or phenic acids.

After the operation, there are two untoward accidents which you may have to meet; first, hemorrhages, and you can understand the reason of this when you think of the active circulation in the liver; then biliary fistula. The hemorrhages are generally venous, and cold injections of perchloride of iron will be likely to control them. The other accident, the creation of a biliary fistula, is not so amenable to treatment, and sometimes patients will carry all their life-long a fistulous tract which gives issue to a more or less free flow of bile.

Thus far I have given exclusive attention to the treatment of hepatitis, and have shown you how rare this affection is in our climate; this is, unfortunately, not the case with another form of inflammation of the hepatic gland, interstitial hepatitis which you will frequently observe in our

wards, and which is known under the name of cirrhosis.*

To any one who should deny the important ad-
vances which histology has made in the study of diseases, I know of no more-convincing instance of such
progress than this subject of cirrhosis. At the commencement of my studies, thirty years ago, we were
taught with reference to cirrhosis the doctrine of
Laénnec, *i. e.*, the existence of two substances in the
liver, a yellow substance and a red substance; the pre-
dominance of the first over the second constituting
cirrhosis.

Since then, thanks to the progress of histology,
we have learned that there are varieties of cirrhosis,

---

* Laënnec was the first to describe cirrhosis as a special
disease; he gave it the name of *cirrhus* (red), and considered
the granulations seen on sections of the liver as productions of
a parasitic nature similar to tubercules, and called these granulations *cirrhoses*. Andral taught the existence of two substances
in the liver, and while the one, the red vascular substance,
undergoes atrophy, the yellow glandular substance hypertro-
phies. Becquerel, in 1840, defended from an anatomo-pathological point of view the correctness of this division of the
liver into two substances. Gubler, in 1853, called attention to
the researches made by Kiernan in England, and Hallmann in
Prussia, and was the first to point out the true nature of cirrhosis.

Lastly, we are especially indebted to Charcot, who in
these latter years has insisted on the importance of periphlebitis as the point of departure of interstitial hepatitis.

which are all characterized by a chronic inflammation
having for its origin the different constituent elements
of the liver. First, we have the common cirrhosis,
dependent on inflammation and hyperplasia of the
capsule of Glisson which surrounds the veins, and this
is the only kind of which I shall speak here. Then
we have a chronic inflammation having for origin the
biliary canaliculi, the hypertrophic cirrhosis of which
I spoke in my last lecture. The lymphatics, as
Hayem, has shown, may also be the point of departure
of a chronic inflammation which is observed in individuals affected with syphilis. This is syphilitic cirrhosis; lastly, according to Talamon the arterial system
may, in its turn, be the origin of this chronic inflammation, and certain forms of hepatic cirrhosis may be
attributed to that arterio-sclerosis of which interstitial
nephritis, as we shall see later, is one of the most common symptoms.

As you see, gentlemen, sclerous inflammation of
the liver may have for its origin the veins, the lymphatics, and the bile ducts, and to each one of these
kinds corresponds a special cirrhosis; if I add that
these lesions may be combined, and constitute mixed
forms, you will agree with me that a great deal has
been accomplished the last fifty years in elucidating
the pathology of the cirrhoses.

Common cirrhosis, which is still called atrophic
cirrhosis, is constituted, as I just told you, by hyperplasia of the connective tissue frame work of the liver,

which chokes the hepatic cells and compresses the capillary venous net work; we know also that this interstitial inflammation has for its starting point the ramifications of the portal vein, and it is in the cellular tissue which surrounds these veins, *i. e.* in Kiernan's interlobular spaces, that the inflammatory processes begin.

This is of great importance from the point of view of the pathogeny of cirrhosis: it explains the well known action of the alcohols on the development of this affection, a cause which is so frequent, that in England the name of " gin drinkers' liver " is given to this disease. The alcohol, absorbed from the surface of the digestive tube by the venous system, passes to the liver, but its presence in the ramifications of the portal vein determines a periphlebitis of special nature, which propagates itself in the connective tissue bindweb of the liver, and determines there that particular hyperplasia which characterizes cirrhosis. Inasmuch as drinking habits have been for several years on the increase (and here in Paris as well as in other parts of the world)—moreover, as in consequence of the high price of wine and the ravages of the phylloxera the alcohols of vinous origin are becoming so rare that only the rich can afford them, so that the fiery liquors are chiefly in demand and the poorer qualities of distilled spirits sold in the dram shops are consumed by the masses, it is easy to understand the reason of the constantly increasing number of cases of alcoholic cirrhosis.

These two conditions, the growing abuse of alcoholic stimulants and the use of impure spirits, sufficiently explain the increasing frequency of cirrhosis, and we have always in our wards one or two typical cases of this affection.

However, in the experiments which I undertook with Audigé on swine, which we subjected to slow poisoning by daily doses of different kinds of alcohols, we did not succeed after three years of experimentation in engendering interstitial hepatitis. It will not do to conclude from the negative result of these experiments that alcohol is not influential in the production of cirrhosis, for the anatomical arrangement of the liver in swine explains the absence of cirrhosis in the particular cases referred to, the liver in hogs being extraordinarily supplied with connective tissue reticulum, which keeps the lobules apart and prevents their compression.*

You all know the train of symptoms which cirrhotic patients present when they enter the hospital:

---

* In our experimental researches on chronic alcoholism practised for three years on a number of hogs, we noted the following symptoms: During life some of the animals under experimentation presented a yellowish coloration of the conjunctivæ, and their urine became icteric. This icterus always showed itself when we exceeded the quantity of two grams per kilogram of the animal's weight, and the symptoms were more marked with alcohols of bad quality (the higher atomic alcohols) than with ethylic alcohol. At the autopsy we found

ascites more or less developed, abundant serous diarrhœa, hemorrhoids, enlargement of the abdominal
veins, advanced cachexia, profound emaciation, high-
colored urine, liver generally reduced in size, spleen,
however, somewhat tumefied. Such are the morbid
phenomena observed in such cases, all resulting from
the mechanical disturbance in the circulation of the
portal vein. It is this mechanical disturbance, having
its origin in the intra-hepatic reticulum, which has for
its consequence stasis of blood in the portal vein and
mesenteric veins, this stasis entailing effusion of serum
into the abdominal cavity, preventing absorption from
the surface of the intestinal mucosa, and thus giving
rise to serous diarrhœa and hemorrhoids. It is to
overcome this obstacle that the spleen augments in
size, and it is to establish a supplementary circulation
that the subcutaneous abdominal circulation undergoes increased development.

But what we have just been considering is but
the ultimate stage of the disease; there is another

---

nothing but congestion of the liver; in certain cases the hepatic
parenchyma was friable, but there was neither interstitial
hepatitis nor ascites.

Prof. Cornil, who made the histological examination of
the liver in the poisoned animals, indeed noticed an extraordin-
ary amount of connective tissue substance, but this is, he says,
a normal condition in the hog. (See Beaumetz and Audigé,
" Experiments in Chronic Alcohol-Poisoning," (translation of
E. P. Hurd), in Therapeutic Gazette for July and August, 1884).

stage which precedes the organization of the connective web-work, a congestive period during which the patient does not demand medical help. He, in fact, does not present himself at the hospital till his disease has produced ascites, and only applies for treatment when it is too late for anything but palliation.

In these sclerous, interstitial inflammations, we can only influence the congestive element which precedes the connective tissue hyperplasia. What I say to you of the liver, I may also say of interstitial nephritis, of sclerous myelitis, of which the inflammatory process is the same. When once the proliferation of connective tissue cells is a settled fact, we can not by any therapeutic means destroy these organized products, or hope to restore the hepatic cells when we have to do with the liver, the malphigian bodies, when we have to do with the kidney, or the nerve tubes when it is a case of interstitial myelitis.

We can then hope to render efficacious service only in the first period of the disease, characterized by congestive symptoms; hence, in the case of every person addicted to alcoholic abuses, you should give your attention to even the minor symptoms referable to the liver, and combat them by the best means available for diminishing hyperæmia of the liver, *i. e.*, revulsives, cholagogues, milk diet, and absolute abstinence from alcoholic beverages. By these means you will sometimes obtain really marvellous results, and one of the most curious cases which I have ever witnessed was that of a patient who was sent to me by Dr. Tourangin, and who presented all the symptoms of advanced cirrhosis; he is to-day quite well, and has been so for more than two years.*

You will place, then, at the head of your treatment, milk diet which is capable of itself of bringing about an amelioration equivalent to a cure; and you may have seen by recent discussions at the Medical Society of the Hospitals that such cases are not as rare as one would think.

You may add a therapeutic agent which I have tried, and which has given me good results; I refer to the hippurate of lime, which you may prescribe according to the following formula:

R   Pure hippuric acid, 25 grams,
    Milk of lime, (to neutralize) q. s.,
    Syrup, 500. grams,
    Essence of anise (to flavor) q. s.
M.   Sig.—Four to six spoonfuls a day.

---

* The following are the notes of this case: M. R., watchmaker, aged 44 years, of somewhat intemperate habits, which he had contracted during the siege of Paris.

This man was in an advanced state of cachexia, the liver was voluminous and irregular, urine small in quantity and high colored; he had diarrhœa and was emaciating so rapidly that we at first thought it a case of cancer of the liver making rapid progress.

This patient was subjected to milk diet, and blisters were applied over the hepatic region. After six months of treatment he got completely well, and has kept well ever since.

But it will not do to place more than a moderate confidence in this medicament, and you will be often fated to see your patients improve in health only to resume their alcoholic excesses, and to succumb to the progress of their cirrhosis.

Do you ask whether, when cirrhosis has attained its complete development, there is nothing to be done ? There will certainly be a demand for medical help, and there is much that you can do in the way of combating the mechanical troubles effected in the portal circulation, and in particular the ascites which results therefrom.

Is it then possible by diuretics or purgatives to cause the ascites to disappear ?

This is the opinion of some authorities, who believe that they find in cirrhosis an indication for the anti-hydropical (evacuant) medication of which I spoke while on diseases of the heart.* I do not hold this view, and I maintain that in the majority of cases, diuretics, and especially purgatives, have no effect in removing the abdominal effusion, and when you continue these medicines too long, for reasons obvious enough, you injure rather than improve the state of your patient. I think, then, that after a few moderate trials it is better to discontinue diuretics and drastics.

---

*Diseasés of the Heart, Vol. I, p. 83, (Ed. of G. S. Davis, Detroit).

Is it desirable to resort to tapping ?

Here, also, there is much dispute. In most cases, and I have only to call your attention to what takes place before your own eyes in our wards, you will see that tapping, in the true cirrhotic, instead of prolonging life, only hastens the end; hence I remain generally deaf to the entreaties of my patients, and put off this operation as long as possible, and only perform it in the last stages, when the patients are becoming asphyxiated by reason of the enormous development of the abdomen. This custom, gentlemen, is not peculiar to myself, but quite as much characterizes the practice of a great number of my colleagues.

The annals of medicine, however, contain some curious cases in which patients have been known to hold out for months, even for years, owing to tappings frequently repeated, and even recoveries have been reported by this means.

The number of recoveries is greater than one would think. In the discussion which took place in 1885 on this subject at the Medical Society of the Hospitals, a large number of our colleagues related facts of this kind, and Lancereaux, in a communication made in 1886, cited still other examples.

I have myself published an interesting observation of a patient affected with alcoholic cirrhosis, who was tapped and got well, continuing so for three months, till, by an imprudence, he contracted pneumonia and died. The autopsy enabled us to confirm our diagnosis, interstitial hepatitis being found.*

There is, then, a question of opportuneness, which must first be settled. In certain cases, in fact, the cirrhosis affects only a limited portion of the hepatic gland, and if the patient, by an intelligent hygiene, by absolute abstinence from alcoholic drinks, succeeds in arresting the invading march of the hepatic sclerosis, it is easy to understand that, by the fact of the oozing of liquid from the veins being slow and in small quantity, or even arrested altogether (owing to a sufficient supplementary venous circulation), paracentesis practiced in due time may free the abdomen, favor the portal circulation, and put the patient in a better situation.

On the other hand, when the cirrhosis is complete, tapping can be only palliative, and the obstruction to the circulation remaining, the abdomen speedily fills again with the liquid effusion, and thus the blood is drained of a large quantity of its serum; it stands to reason, then, that this abundant serous blood-letting will enfeeble, if it does not quickly kill your patient already cachectic.

How are you to judge of the opportuneness of paracentesis? If you have to do with a young, vigorous patient, if the digestive functions are performed

* Dujardin-Beaumetz on "The Treatment of Cirrhosis" (Soc. Med. des Hôp., 1886).

with sufficient regularity, if the nutrition is not too profoundly disturbed, your duty is to tap, and to watch and see if there is more or less speedy reproduction of the liquid.   If the abdomen speedily refills after three or four days, recovering its former distention, it will not do to repeat the tapping.   If, on the contrary, the patient has derived benefit for a fortnight, three weeks, or a month, from the paracentesis, you may repeat the operation.

But when the cirrhotic patient is very cachectic, when his emaciation is considerable, when assimilation is nil, or almost so, I believe that if you desire to prolong the life of your patient, you should not perform tapping.

The economy becomes habituated, in a certain measure, to the often enormous accumulation of liquid in the abdomen, till little by little the patient becomes enfeebled and succumbs to the cachexia.

As for the rules which should govern you in the performance of paracentesis abdominalis, I will not take up this subject, for it is, as you know, one of the most simple and easy of operations; at the same time I will call your attention to two points: First of all, you should be careful as to the place where you make your trocar-puncture, in order to avoid wounding the enlarged and distended veins, which in the cirrhotic ramify so abundantly upon the abdominal wall.   Then, when the tapping is terminated, you should see that the patient lies on the side opposite to that where the puncture was made, and that he keeps this position for some time, in order to enable the wound which you have made to cicatrize. You thus avoid those fistulæ which often remain behind, and which are exceedingly disagreeable, for they soil the patient's linen and produce cutaneous inflammation.

Apart from this interesting question of paracentesis, are there any other indications for the treatment of cirrhosis? I know of none that are very clear, with the exception of milk diet, whereby, in fact, you may be able to augment the quantity of urine, support the patient, and prolong his life. This is indeed very little, but, I repeat, this very paucity of therapeutic resources results from the profound disorders effected in the hepatic gland, disorders which are always beyond the reach of any medicinal treatment. I shall finish what pertains to the treatment of diseases of the liver by devoting a lecture to hydatid cysts of this organ.

CHAPTER VII.

TREATMENT OF HYDATID CYSTS OF THE LIVER.

SUMMARY:—Tænia Echinococcus—Development of Hydatid Cysts—Prophylactic Treatment—Frequency of Hydatid Cysts in Iceland—Diagnosis of Hydatid Cysts—Medical Treatment—Iodide of Potassium—Electro-Puncture—Capillary Punctures—Aspiration—Results Given—Free Opening of the Sac—Methods of Begin, Recamier and Jobert—Resumé of Treatment—Lavages of the Sac.

Hydatid cysts may develop in all the tissues of the economy, and if I here occupy your time with the treatment of these cysts, it is because it is in the liver that they are most frequently observed. But before touching upon the therapeutics of hydatid tumors, it is necessary that I should state as briefly as possible their pathogeny. When, in my "Diseases of the Stomach and Intestines"* I traced the history of the tæniæ, I mentioned that these cestoids, before reaching the stage of tape worm, pass through an intermediate vesicular stage—that of cysticercus. These are facts long known in respect to animals; we may add that man may be the bearer of these vesicular worms, and without dwelling upon the cysticerci of the tænia, which have been known to develop in

---

Wm. Wood & Co., N. Y., Chap. xxv p. 360.

12 I

the muscles of man,* and which render him *measly*, (a condition once supposed to be peculiar to the hog), I wish to call your attention to another verminous affection, unhappily more frequent, and which is also one of the phases of the life of a tænia, I refer to the *echinococcus cyst.*

It is in the dog or the wolf that we find the tænia echinococcus. This worm is very different from those I have described; it is extremely small, scarcely appreciable to the naked eye, and is composed of a head furnished with four suckers, a double crown of hooks, and a body formed of three rings, of which the last only is provided with genital organs. This tænia produces eggs in abundance which are found in the fæcal matters of these animals.

Suppose now that these excrementitious matters are washed by the rain and carried to a brook or spring, and an individual drinks this water: the ova will be absorbed, will penetrate the intestinal walls into the abdominal venous system, and will thus enter the general circulation. They will then engender in various organs, but particularly in the liver, through which filters all the blood of the portal vein, liquid tumors more or less voluminous, which have been described under the name of *hydatid cysts.* You all are familiar with these vesicles of variable size, having the aspect of a trembling jelly, and containing a

---

* Delpech, Lancereaux, Davaine, Boyron.

transparent non-albuminous saline liquid; these are the *acephalocysts* described by Laënnec.

If you examine carefully the walls of these cysts, you will find them composed of a series of structure-less layers imbricating each other, the most internal of which presents a granular aspect, concerning which Prof. Charles Robin has given a long description. It is, in fact, the germinal membrane, and if you observe it with care, you will find sticking to its surfaces, or floating in the liquid, little white grains, which micros-copical examination will enable you to recognize as constituted by a body formed of a roundish vesicle containing granules of carbonate and phosphate of lime. These vesicles, the anterior part of which is constituted by a head absolutely identical with that of the tænia echinococcus, *i. e.*, presenting a double crown of hooks and four suckers, are the *scolices* of this tænia, and if by accident these echinococci are swallowed by a wolf or dog, they engender in this ani-mal the tæniæ of which I have just spoken.

Von Siebold in 1853 gave to twelve young dogs and to a fox some echinococci from the lungs of an ox and a sheep, and he found in the small intestine a great number of little tape worms. Von Beneden made similar experiments, and obtained like results. These experiments were successfully repeated in 1863 by Finsen and Krabb.

Pardon me, gentlemen, for having dwelt so long on the development of these hydatids, but I have seen so many mistakes committed in this connection, and witnessed such confusion of opinion on this subject,

that I deem it necessary to state briefly and clearly
what is known relative to this matter of pathogeny.
Moreover, as you will see, important conclusions from
the point of view of the prophylactic treatment of
hydatid cysts result from the knowledge of the facts
which I have stated.   But before going further, I wish
to say a few words concerning the ultimate course of
these hydatid cysts, which may present themselves in
all parts of the economy; but as their seat of predilec-
tion is assuredly the liver, I intend to confine my
remarks to the hydatid cysts of this organ.

Enclosed in a firm resisting fibrous envelope—a
true adventitious cyst—these hydatids tend gradually
to increase in size, and this increase ultimately produces rupture of the cyst into the neighboring organs.
If into the peritoneum, death is the consequence; if
into the veins, into the vena cava for instance, a fatal
embolism is the result; if the cyst bursts into the pleura
and lungs, you readily understand the grave consequences of such perforation.

The most favorable cases are those in which the
sac ruptures into the stomach or intestine, and this is
one of the modes of cure.

I have just said that the bursting of the cyst into
the peritoneum is fatal. This does not always hold
true, and several cases are on record of hydatid cysts
which have opened into the peritoneum, and in which
recovery took place after a sharp attack of peritonitis.
The best instance of the kind to which I can refer is

that of a young girl, five months pregnant, who entered our wards; she presented a fine example of hydatid cyst of the liver. We tapped her and drew off 1,500 grams of liquid; two months after she fell upon the sidewalk and ruptured the cyst; there was, as she told us at the time, the sensation of a liquid effused into the abdominal cavity. A frightful peritonitis ensued, a miscarriage took place, and in the end she recovered.

These cysts may, however, disappear without bursting into the neighboring organs; the hydatids die, the liquid is reabsorbed, leaving behind nothing but a mass of fatty debris representing the regressive metamorphoses that the sac has undergone, and at the autopsy these remains will be found.

In other circumstances, the sac suppurates without undergoing rupture, and the patient succumbs to the progress of the putrid infection determined by the suppuration. Lastly, in some cases, without bursting into neighboring organs, without suppurating, these cysts may cause death by the cachectic state to which the patients are reduced by reason of disturbances in the functions of the digestive tube effected by pressure of the tumor.

Hence, then, the rarity of spontaneous recovery, the possibility of the cyst bursting into neighboring organs with either death or recovery, frequent suppuration of the sac, profound disorders of nutrition— all this goes to show that hydatid cyst of the liver is a

grave affection, necessitating active and energetic interference.

I will first consider the prophylactic treatment.
Our knowledge of the mode of evolution of the tænia
itself suggests what this should be, and I can not too
much impress upon you the danger, when in the country, of drinking directly from brooks or springs, as
these water-sources are so apt to be contaminated by
the ova of the tænia voided by animals and carried
there by the rain. It is important, then, for the
soldier as well as for the laboring man, for the peas-
ant as well as for the traveller, never to drink water
from springs or pools without having first filtered it
(through a charcoal filter, for instance) or boiled it,
for when once the disease is contracted, it becomes a
serious matter to get rid of it.

There is one country where these precautions
ought to be rigorously carried out, viz.: in Iceland,
where hydatid cysts are extremely frequent. According to Dr. Hyatalin, one-tenth of the population of
this island are affected with hydatid cysts; but this
figure is too high, if we may rely on the statistics of
Finsen and Jonassen, which show that $\frac{1}{36}$th of the
population (viz.: about 2,300) are victims of echinococcus.*

---

*Iceland is, moreover, the true country of the vesicular
helminthi or cestoid worms. The sheep have almost all stag-
gers, produced by the tænia coenurus, and out of 100 dogs

This sad condition results from the following circumstances: First, in Iceland the dogs are very numerous; 20,000 dogs to 70,000 inhabitants; then a great many of the animals that graze are affected with hydatid cysts. When these beasts are slaughtered, it is the custom to throw their entrails to the dogs, the dogs thereby contract tænia, and as they live in terms of close intimacy with the inhabitants, and deposit their excrements on the snow near the farms or *boers*, it results that when the snow melts, animals as well as man that consume a great deal of lichen, devour the eggs of the tænia which have been deposited thereon, and thus contract hydatid cysts. So, in order to combat this vicious circle, which brings this result that the frequency of tænia in the dog entails frequency of hydatid cysts in men and other animals, and *vice versa*, Murchison thinks that this sanitary regulation should be enforced, viz.: the dogs should be absolutely prevented from eating the entrails or debris of animals near the slaughter houses; then they should be fed only with cooked food, and frequently purged to rid them of their tape worms. Galliot proposes also an energetic remedy: to kill all the dogs, and replace

---

Krabbe found 93 infected with different tæniæ, in the following proportions: *tænia marginata*, 75 per cent.; *tænia coenurus*, 18 per cent.; *tænia echinococus*, 28 per cent.; *tænia cumarina*, 57 per cent.; *tænia lagopodis* (of the blue fox). 21 per cent.; *bothriocephalus cuscus*, 5 per cent.; *ascaris marginata*, 2 per cent.

them by others of a different race, which shall be prevented from eating the debris of diseased animals.

But, to return to our subject, supposing that you have a patient affected with cysts of the liver, what are you going to do? The diagnosis, save in exceptional cases, is generally easy, but you must not count too much on a characteristic sign of cyst, the hydatid thrill. This is a rare symptom; the Icelandic physicians, who see so many cases, have never remarked this symptom.

The gradual development of the tumor, its rounded form, and, it may be, the aspiratory puncture, generally make the diagnosis sufficiently certain. But before coming to the subject of tapping, I wish to say a few words concerning the medical treatment.

Certain medicines have been vaunted in the treatment of hydatid cysts. Laënnec advised chloride of sodium; Hyatalin, kamala (in tincture, 30-drop dose, for adults). Guerault claims that cold applied externally gives good results; Hawkins vaunted potassium iodide, and Jaccoud speaks well of this remedy. If, however, we can rely on the authority of Frerichs, this treatment is of no value, for he has never found iodine in the hydatid liquid of individuals taking iodide of potassium. This view, however, has been combated by Semmola, of Naples, who has shown that in certain cases where potassium iodide is given, the iodine may pass into the interior of the cystic pouch.

This is his mode of procedure: he subjects the patient to an iodide treatment, then, at the end of several days, he aspirates the sac and ascertains if iodine appears in the liquid; if it be found there, he continues to give iodide of potash, and claims that he obtains a very considerable diminution in the sac and its reduction to a solid mass; in negative cases, (*i.e.*, where iodine is not found in the water of the sac) he has recourse to other modes of treatment.

Before resorting to puncture, you may employ a therapeutic means which I believe is destined to be very successful; I refer to electrolysis.

In a previous course of lectures * I showed you the good results of electro-punctures in the treatment of aneurisms. The same method is applicable in the treatment of hydated cysts. You enter the cyst with your acupuncture needles, then you connect them with the poles of a galvanic battery. Here the kind of current is not of the same importance as in the case of the aneurismal tumor. You may employ indifferently the positive or negative current, or even both at once. Hilton Fagge and Cooper Foster, who have published eight cases with satisfactory results, employ only the negative current.

I have practiced electrolysis in three cases, and this is my mode of procedure: I place over the cyst,

* Diseases of the Heart, Part II (G. S. Davis, Detroit Series for 1887).

according to the method of Apostoli, a cake of moist clay connected with the negative pole, which terminates in a circular disc resting upon the clay. This clay cake does not touch the needles, two or three of which I introduce into the tumor. These needles are the same as those of which I make use in the electrolysis of aneurisms of the aorta. They are covered with a protective insulating varnish, and the two extremities alone are free. The penetration and extraction of these needles is performed with the same instruments as in aneurismal electro-puncture.* I keep the intensity of the current between 40 and 45 milliampéres, and the duration for each needle averages ten minutes. I have not obtained complete cure by this means, but like Semmola and Gallozi, I have observed marked diminutions in the size of the sac, and have not noticed any untoward results whatever.

Therefore I believe that this method can be an eminently advantageous one. First, of itself it may bring about destruction of the hydatids and their slow resorption, and if it does not produce this effect, it will always tend to produce adhesions between the sac and the abdominal walls, adhesions which, as you know, are conditions of success in these mechanical evacuations of hydatid cysts. This operation, practised with success in England and in Italy, deserves henceforth to be adopted in our country.

---

* See Diseases of the Heart, Part II (Ed. of G. S. Davis), page 285.

We come now to the treatment of hydatid cysts by puncture, an operation which may serve not only as a means of diagnosis, but also as a therapeutic agency, for it may of itself bring about a complete cure in some cases. These punctures are practised with capillary trocars which may be attached to the aspirator. Although Murchison rejects aspiration, and uses only the capillary trocars, it must be admitted that Dieulafoy has rendered to medical practice in general, and to the treatment of hydatid cysts in particular, a great service in making easy and handy the method of aspiration. It is in fact the only method which we ought now to put in usage; but before resorting to aspiration, you should remember that these capillary punctures are not always absolutely safe, as the fatal cases of Moisenett, Pidoux, and Damaschino go to show.

With aspiration, such disasters are however very rare; but in order to avoid all accidents and to obtain from the operation all the success desirable, the following precautions should be taken:

First, to withdraw all liquid from the sac, and to make the aspiration as complete as possible. This is a practice on which Gosselin, Jaccoud, Dieulafoy, Moutard-Martin, and Desnos have rightly insisted, and which is in vogue among the Icelandic physicians.

---

* Murchison, Diseases of the Liver, Dieulafoy, On the Diagnosis and Treatment of Hydatid Cysts. (Traité de l'Aspiration.)

Then, you should not employ the aspirator needles, but always use a trocar of small diameter; in aspirating the sac you may, in fact, with the needle wound certain parts of the sac or the hepatic parenchyma, and determine a hemorrhage or a lesion which shall compromise the result of the operation; this does not happen with the trocar, of which the sharp extremity is withdrawn.

Moreover, it is a good plan to perform aspiration according to the rules of the antiseptic method, *i. e.*, to have the instruments scrupulously clean, and the needles rendered aseptic by subjecting them to strong phenic acid before being used.

Lastly, when the aspiration is completed, you should keep the patient in bed at absolute rest for three or four days, and if any inflammatory symptoms should present themselves, ice bags should be placed over the tumors, as Jaccoud recommends.

These capillary aspiratory punctures have been known to result in a radical cure, and without accepting fully Dieulafoy's statement that this result may be attained seven times out of ten, I can affirm that the number of cases of cysts cured by one or more capillary punctures is very large. Look over the reports of the Bulletin of the Medical Society of the Hospitals, consult the work of Davaine, you will see that Moutard-Martin, Gerin-Roze, Dieulafoy, Constantin Paul, Delens, Archambault, Hayem, Laveran, Lanceraux, Charles Bussard, Massart, etc., have recorded cases of this kind. Gosselin, Jaccoud, Desnos, vaunt the curative action of these capillary punctures, and I have myself observed two cases in which a simple aspiratory puncture brought about a cure.*

One of these was the case of a patient on whom I operated at the Hotel Dieu for an abdominal hydatid cyst; the other was that of a child whom I here show you to-day, and who two years ago underwent a single puncture operation for hydatid cyst of the liver, and the child is to-day perfectly well.

The following notes of these cases may be of interest :

HYDATID CYST OF THE ABDOMEN.

Aspiration—Recovery.—Madam R., aged 30 years had in the right iliac fossa a tumor as large as a child's head, regular and ovoid. Aspiration was performed Feb., 25, 1872, with the No. 2 trocar of the Dieulafoy apparatus. Nearly a quart (900 grammes) of liquid clear as water, without a trace of albumen was removed. Five days later the patient left the hospital, cured. Since this period, till 1879, there was no return of the malady.

The other case is given from the notes of Dr. Paul Boncour.

Paul V., aged 11 years, was admitted to St. Antoine Hospital, during the year 1877. In the epigastric region there was a roundish tumor connected with the liver, and making a perceptible bulging at this point; the digestive functions were a little disturbed by the presence of this tumor; the other functions were normal.

This tumor continued to grow for three months, till Nov. 22, 1877, when Dujardin-Beaumetz performed aspiration and

---

*Dujardin Beaumetz '' On the Value of Aspiration in the Treatment and Diagnosis of Hydatid Cysts.'' Bull. de. Thèrap., Feb. 15, 1873, etc.

withdrew 200 grams (or not quite ½ pint) of a clear limpid liquid containing no albumen. No untoward results followed, and the tumor completely disappeared. The child was brought to the hospital in Nov. 1879 and was presented to the class on the occasion of this lecture; the tumor had not been reproduced.

But it may be asked, when is this operation likely to result in perfect cure. One important element of prognosis is the quality of the cyst liquid, and to this the Icelandic physicians attach a great importance. When the liquid is clear, limpid, containing neither albumen nor pus, one puncture may result in cure, if it is turbid and albuminous, a cure from a single puncture is more doubtful; if it is purulent, cure is next to impossible by this means.*

I myself hold this view, and in a memoir published in 1873 in the Bulletin de Thèrapeutique, I urged the absolute necessity of resorting to methods which shall permit a complete washing out of the sac when the cyst has suppurated, for the capillary puncture is insufficient to prevent putrid resorption. It is necessary,

---

* Jonassen gives the following indications from the state of the cyst liquid.

(a) *Liquid clear* as spring water, without any opalescence if heated, containing therefore no albumen, but some chloride of sodium. Liquid of this character indicates that the cyst is still in the state of development, not having undergone any degeneration or inflammation. The vesicles are living vesicles.

(b) *Liquid turbid*, becoming opalescent if heated. The opalescence indicates the death of the echinococci, whose

then, to interfere energetically; the presence, even, of albumen in the cystic liquid necessitates, according to certain medical authorities, and in particular those of Iceland, a free opening of the sac.

How should you make this opening? Several methods have been proposed; that of Begin consists in incising, layer by layer, the abdominal walls down to the peritoneum, then after having stuffed charpie into the wound, the surgeon waits several days to obtain adhesion between the sac and abdominal wall, after which he incises the tumor. This method is now abandoned; possibly as a result of the progress of antiseptic dressings, it may be again tried with reference to seeing if there may not be thereby obtained sufficient adhesions.

The method of Recamier is still in usage; it consists in opening the sac by caustics. You make successive applications of caustic down to the sac,

---

cadavers, dissolved in the liquid of the cyst, have rendered it albuminous.

(c) *Liquid with purulent aspect*, but not generally containing real pus. This indicates the presence of fatty granules, due to regression of the cadavers of the echinococci. You find in this liquid little albumen, considerable chloride of sodium, and the hooklets of the echinococci, the chitine of which has resisted all the causes of destruction. These two last signs when discovered, indicate without any possible doubt, the presence of a hydatid cyst.

The free opening of the sac, with frequent cleansing lavages, is indicated in the two latter cases.

employing Vienna paste or chloride of zinc; Richet
prefers the latter. Then, when you have reached a
sufficient depth, you plunge in your trocar or your
bistoury, and open the cyst. In these cases, the slough
formed by the caustic ought, as Demarquay has
shown, to be quite extensive; you want a large opening in order to make sufficient and complete lavages
of the sac, and give issue to the numerous hydatids
and their membranes. If you employ the trocar,
select the largest size. My colleague, Ernest Besnier,
has had made at the Maison de Santé an enormous
trocar, of which I make use, and I confess that it was
not without considerable trepidation that I first dared
to plunge this trocar into the cystic tumor. But large
openings have great advantages, and I cannot too
much recommend you to bear this in mind, and not
err on the side of timidity.

Jobert, Dolbeau, and Gallard, in order to obtain
the adhesions so much desired between the abdominal
wall and the sac, have counselled a method which
seems to me to be excellent; it is to leave the trocar-
canula in place for one or two days. The canula prevents the passage of liquid into the abdomen, favors
adhesion, and its presence permits lavage of the sac.

Surgical interference has been much oftener resorted to the last few years in the treatment of hydatid
cysts, owing to the progress of antiseptic methods.
Hence, the processes of Begin and Recamier, which
are confessedly slow and insufficient, have been

abandoned in favor of immediate and free opening of the sac by means of the bistoury. The results obtained by this method have been very satisfactory. The large opening gives easy exit to all hydatids, and enables one to empty and wash out the sac. The brilliant success obtained by Lawson Tait in the case of one of our most noted faculty professors by this method has tended to make this operation popular in our country.

Hence, to sum up, I would say: If you have to do with a hydatid cyst, make an aspiratory puncture and empty completely the sac with the trocar. If the liquid is limpid and the sac is single, you may hope for a cure, though you may have to repeat the puncture. If the liquid is turbid and albuminous or purulent, you may have to resort to some other operation. You may then have recourse to the surgical procedure which I have mentioned, *i. e.*, free opening of the sac with the knife, or to some of the ancient methods by caustics, following the rules which Davaine has laid down.* If you resort to the caustic, when the eschar has attained a sufficient depth, plunge in a large trocar, then withdraw it, leaving the canula in place for two or three days; then, for the canula, you may substitute a rubber drainage tube, and perform frequent washings of the sac.

---

*Davaine, Traitement des Entozoaires, 2d. Ed., 1878, p. 662.

13 x

These lavages are very necessary, and ought to be made with antiseptic liquids, such as solutions of phenic acid, boric acid or alcohol. Boinet recommends iodine; Ludet, Cadet-de-Gassicourt, and Dolbeau highly recommend the employment of bile, basing themselves on cases of spontaneous cure of the cyst by the opening of a bile duct into it. Pavy has counselled injections of ethereal extract of male fern; and I cannot too much urge the use of a solution of chloral, 1 to 200, and the washing out of the sac with it morning and evening. You can also use all the other antiseptic solutions, boric acid, thymic acid, phenol, etc.

Do not forget, at the same time, that the walls of the sac may absorb the medicinal solutions with extreme rapidity, and I have often seen carbolic solutions injected into the sac cause a blackening of the urine and real toxic symptoms. This is why you ought not to think of using solutions of red iodide or bichloride of mercury, which are powerfully antiseptic, but which are dangerous by becoming toxic if absorbed in too great quantity.

There are several ways of introducing these antiseptic solutions into the sac. Revelliod, of Geneva, suggests employing in these cases the syphon. He introduces into the sac a long rubber tube communicating with a basin, which the patient may raise or lower at will, and which, according to the position which he takes, enables the liquid to flow into the cyst or flow out from it.

I have tried this method of syphoning, and confess that I have not derived the same advantages therefrom as my confrère of Geneva claims, since, for various reasons, the syphon does not always work to your satisfaction. In order to inject my antiseptic solutions, I employ either a common syringe or, what is better, one of those handy apparatuses which are applied to bottles; by simply compressing a rubber ball injector, you can aspirate the liquid contained in the bottle, and a rubber tube furnished with a canula enables you to direct the current upon any point or into any cavity that you desire.

But it must be admitted that the difficulty of antiseptic cleansings in the treatment of hydatid cysts of the liver is due, in the majority of cases, to the obstacles in the way of the discharge of the echinococci by the abdominal opening, and you have seen a recent case in our female wards illustrative of this fact, where, despite the large extent which we gave to this opening, the exit of the hydatid sacs was rendered extremely difficult.* You must then take the utmost pains to keep this opening as wide and free as possible, and if it ·contracts, you should not hesitate an instant to dilate and enlarge it by means of a sea tangle tent.

---

* A large trocar was used, but it kept getting clogged. By phenic acid lavages the debris were finally cleared, and the patient got well.

Do not forget, moreover, after each dressing to withdraw the sound which you have introduced by the opening. Often the orifice of the sound is clogged by the cyst membranes, which easily obliterate the bore of the tube, and if you withdraw the canula, you see a gush of putrid matters issuing by your fistulous opening.

The sac retracts little by little, and you find yourselves able to get less and less of liquid into it by your syringe; you take a smaller tube, and after a while no more liquid can be made to enter. You take out the tube, and the patient is cured. Recovery is not always the rule. Often the patient succumbs to the suppuration, or, as in a case that I saw with Dr. Herard, when in a lobe of the liver one sac has disappeared, another develops in another lobe. But whatever may happen, you should do everything, try everything— when once the cyst has been opened—to avoid the causes of septicæmia, and to support the strength of the patient by an appropriate treatment.

As you see, the treatment of hydatid cysts of the liver demands surgical knowledge and skill. But it belongs to you, as practitioners of medicine, to be ready for the emergency and to employ the needed surgical means, and no less responsibility belongs to the after-care of the case, which demands constant watchfulness and attention, so that it may be said that the treatment of this affection is as much the province of the physician as of the surgeon.

INDEX.

— 183 —

PAGE.

www.ingramcontent.com/pod-product-compliance
Lightning Source LLC
Chambersburg PA
CBHW031105020726
47495CB00007B/2058